The Purples

MW01703336

The Purples

John North Jr.

NPI

Northwest Publishing, Inc.
Salt Lake City, Utah

The Purples

All rights reserved.
Copyright © 1994 John North Jr.

Reproductions in any manner, in whole or in part,
in English or in other languages, or otherwise
without written permission of the publisher is prohibited.
This is a work of fiction.

For information address: Northwest Publishing,
6906 South 300 West, Salt Lake City, Utah 84047
JC 06 24 94

PRINTING HISTORY
First Printing 1994

ISBN: 1-56901-187-7

NPI books are published by Northwest Publishing Incorporated,
6906 South 300 West, Salt Lake City, Utah 84047.
The name "NPI" and the "NPI" logo are trademarks belonging to
Northwest Publishing Incorporated.

PRINTED IN THE UNITED STATES OF AMERICA.
10 9 8 7 6 5 4 3 2 1

Dedication

To Olie…one whom I will never forget.
To Doug…who would always listen.
To Gina…always ready to give a hand.
To Jean…willing to help with words.

Table of Contents

The Prohibition Era

No person shall, on or after the date when the 18th Amendment to the constitution of the United States goes into effect, manufacture, sell, barter, transport, import, export, deliver, furnish or possess any intoxicating liquor except as authorized in this act.

Title II, Section 3, National Prohibition Act

With these measured words was born one of the most lurid periods of American history. Prohibition, the Roaring Twenties, Al Capone, speakeasies, moonshiners, bootleggers, cocktails and the gangster's moll as style setter were the offspring of this venture into enforced sobriety. Saloons, where "decent" women had once entered only to reclaim errant husbands or sons, became nightclubs, haunt of the scions, both male and female, of the best families. Every family of wealth had a preferred bootlegger, and this individual was as much a member of the social support system as the personal physician or family grocer.

As the criminal class entered general society, so, too, did the violence that inevitably accompanies lawless activity. While every metropolitan area had its share of murder and mayhem, Chicago became infamous for its gangsters and gangsterism, as well as for the dubious integrity of its law enforcement officials. To this day, Capone, his minions and the St. Valentine's Day Massacre are associated with the City of Big Shoulders and environs.

The story that follows is fiction, although in some parts names, dates and places are gangland history. One of the most notorious mobster gangs during the Prohibition Era was better known as the "Purple Gang."

One

The Purple Gang's Hideout

Big Fish Inn
Ellsworth, Michigan

It was a dark and rainy February night when Abe Bernstein was coming in the side entrance of the old two-story building, a hunting and fishing lodge that had gone out of business years back. They called it the Big Fish Inn. It had a large hotel close to the water's edge and a few old log cabins scattered here and there over the grounds with tall pine trees surrounding the property.

It was an ideal location for Abe and his Purple Gang to hide out after pulling off a big job downstate, especially since the Inn was about 200 miles northwest of Detroit, where the Purple Mob had their permanent headquarters.

Abe always liked this place for it suited his needs when it was time to run and seclude from the law.

The Inn was located geographically in a hollow area just off the main highway, hidden from everything and everyone—a thickly wooded area on the shores of a chain of lakes, close to Lake Michigan, just outside a little town called Ellsworth, Michigan.

As Abe hurriedly walked up to the huge stone fireplace in the main lobby of the hotel to get warm, he unstrapped the holster harness from around his chest and said, “Phil, ya know I got a message from Scarface last night.”

“What d’ya mean?” Phil answered.

“He wants to borrow you and your brother Harry for a job coming up on Valentine’s Day. It’s a big one!” Abe said.

“Anything you say, Abe. You’re the boss of this outfit,” replied Phil.

The mob huddled around the fire, as most of them were wet and cold. They had just come in from a long, cold night on the road from Detroit, after eluding the police from a hijacking job. Coming off the old highway that goes into Ellsworth, they blew a tire on their new ’29 Studebaker. They had to change tires fast because they didn’t want any unwanted onlookers to spot them. It was one of those nights when the rain was an unbearable mist and fog. Just plain wet and cold. They put the spare tire on and headed for the entrance to the winding drive that would lead them up to the Big Fish Inn. They were all soaking wet, and a warm fire in the fireplace would feel very comforting.

Prior to their arriving at the Inn, Sheila, Abe’s girlfriend, who was living at the Inn, had everything ready for their arrival—hot food cooking in the kitchen and a good, hot fire going in the old fireplace. Sheila was a local girl in her early 20s with long, black, silky hair and brown eyes. Her long, well-built body was more than enough to excite any man. What a doll!

Sheila was not too well respected in the village. The villagers knew of her past. Her parents were long gone when she turned fourteen. Her mother was in a state mental institution and her father was a drunk, living somewhere in Charlevoix, a city fifty miles north of Ellsworth. Charlevoix was a millionaire's playland for downstate big shots to escape to for the summer.

Sheila was always hanging around the local pubs and taverns just up the hill from the Inn, where the center of town was. Abe took a liking to her quite some time ago. He made her his possession when he was at the Big Fish. Sheila was being used by Abe, but she didn't care. It was a far cry from what her earlier life was like. Abe treated her like a queen most of the time, just to keep her satisfied. When he would come to the Inn to hide out, he always brought her expensive jewelry or a high-priced gift of some kind. Fortunately, these items were not hard to come by for the gang had quite a surplus of such items in storage from all their robberies and hijacking jobs.

Sheila snuggled up to Abe by the fireplace and said, "Abe, honey, what did you bring for your baby this trip?"

Nonchalantly, he replied, "Baby, you just go out there in that new Studebaker and open up the trunk. You'll find a big black box in there. You bring it in here and show the boys! Okay?"

Hurriedly, Sheila ran outside and quickly was back inside. As she opened the big box, all the gang stood around the fire with eagerness, because they knew how Sheila loved expensive gifts.

In seconds, Sheila had the box open and was pulling out a beautiful long silver ermine coat.

She sighed for a moment, and Abe said, "Come on, Sheila, put it on. Everybody wants to see how you look in it."

As the light from the crackling fire was flashing onto her body, Sheila slipped into the coat. What a knockout!

Abe said, "Ya know, honey, you could pass for Greta Garbo."

Sheila loved the compliment and ran upstairs to fix herself up for the evening. Abe always wanted her to look good the first night.

As she was running up the stairs, Abe shouted, "Be sure and wear that classy looking coat tonight. We're going to take a run up to Charlevoix. There's a new club up there by the lake that the boys and I want to check out."

Sheila said, "I'll be right down after I change dresses. I want to put on that red dress you always liked—the one that shines and sparkles like little diamonds!"

Abe got the message and, with a glimmer in his eyes, immediately followed Sheila upstairs. Abe entered the bedroom just as Sheila was slipping off her dress. As Sheila was standing in front of the big mirror, Abe could not resist the temptation to touch and kiss her. They made love for about an hour. Later they joined Phil and Harry in the lobby.

They checked their pistols in their holsters. Abe always carried a .45 automatic. His father gave it to him when he was a young boy. He was proud of his dad and was always talking about his being in the war and everything over in France.

Phil went outside into the drizzly night and started up the car.

Abe said, "George, you stay here tonight and be the watch dog. Look, if there's anything wrong when we get back, be sure to give us the signal as we hit the entrance to the Inn. And George, you know the number at the club. Give me a call about midnight, okay?"

"Don't worry about a thing, Abe. I've got everything covered back here," George said.

George Lewis was the right man to stay behind, for George was the best protector in the gang. He was smart and knew exactly what to do in case of an emergency—kill!

The Purples along with Sheila took off into the dark and dreary night heading for Charlevoix. It was a bad night to travel with the roads dark and slippery from the drizzle, although none of them seemed to mind because they were young, restless and excited, especially since they were heading for this new night spot that Abe had had on his mind for some time.

Sheila sat in the middle, between Phil and Abe. Phil was driving, and Harry took the back seat. Harry always took the back seat because he sat shotgun on every job they pulled.

Harry knew his back-seat job very well and had all his hardware in one suitcase: two Thompson submachine guns, two sawed-off shotguns and an assortment of small arms. Yes, Harry was the head corporal of the firearms department for the Purple Gang.

After an hour of driving, they were getting closer to the outskirts of Charlevoix.

Phil had something on his mind. Finally, he said, "Abe, is Fred Burke going to be at this club tonight?"

"He sure is, Phil. That's the reason we're going up there," Abe replied.

Abe had talked to Al Capone, the big general in Detroit, prior to their escape to the Big Fish Inn. Things in general in the mob world were getting frustrating to the big shots like Al Capone, Dutch Shultz, Jack McGurn and the rest of the Mafia generals scattered throughout the big cities. All the Mafia families were trying to rub out each other to gain supremacy within their own ranks.

Besides that, the big crime fighters—the high judges and the government's F.B.I.—were beginning an era of closing in on all the mobsters throughout the country. Some judges were beginning to slap $100,000 bail bonds on criminals that would eventually send them to jail. These judges were starting to stand up against the Mafia's terrorism and win cases. J. Edgar Hoover and his racket-busters were coming into fame. You could not buy them off anymore and the big generals knew this. That's why Abe was so anxious to have his private meeting with two hoods from Capone's mob.

The generals had to stick together and become more closely knitted. There wasn't room for so many hoods getting a piece of the pie, particularly in Chicago where it was a vast hoodlum's empire of gambling, vice and corruption. The generals were well aware that they had to perform favors for each other.

Abe was about to perform one of these favors within the next week or so. It would be a favor of brotherly love, from one mob leader to another. Al Capone was to be the number one crime boss in Chicago, nobody else—nobody!

Bugsy Moran was moving in on Capone's territory; Scarface did not like it one damn bit. They battled each other with a compulsive fury of passion. It had to come to an end.

"There it is," shouted Phil, "the Cat Club!"

Colored lights blinked all the way around the building. It was not a fancy place from the outside. It had a large outdoor pavilion in back that reached all the way out to the shores of Lake Michigan.

Phil pulled in the parking lot, staying close to the highway because Abe was not taking any chances—they might have to exit rather quickly.

As they walked up to the main bar, the bartender, a big burly-looking fellow, said, "What'll it be, people?"

"Three straight highballs," Abe requested, "and no cheap stuff either!"

People inside were drinking and gambling. It was a far cry from Prohibition, as though it didn't even exist. Money changed hands as fast as the eye could blink. No wonder there were so many young mobsters trying to muscle in on each other. Just too much easy money to be taken from the victim's pockets. They even had a jazz band playing. Gene Krupa was seated behind the drums. It was the roaring '20s and anything went.

Abe asked the bartender if Jack was there.

"Jack McGurn?" he asked.

"Yeah, that's the guy," Abe said.

"He's in the back room. They have a big game going on," the bartender replied.

"Go tell him that Abe wants to talk—and do it now," said the determined leader of the Purple Mob.

Once getting the message from the bartender, Jack got up from the game and came out to welcome them. He took one quick look at Sheila, sighed a little and said, "Son of a bitch, Abe! It sure is good to see ya again. It's been a long time, remember? Remember, Abe?!" Jack said with a happy tone in his voice.

"Yeah, I remember, Jack. We were just little rats then," Abe replied.

"Come on, let's all of us go upstairs and we'll have a little chat, okay?" Jack said.

As they entered a small, poorly lit room, Abc pulled his automatic out of his holster. So did Phil immediately after he saw Abe reach for his pistol. Abe ordered Jack to put on a brighter light.

"Don't worry, Abe. The only guy in here is a buddy of Phil's," said Jack.

As the light went on, lo and behold, it was Phil's old friend from across the river at Windsor.

"Fred Burke! What d'ya know? God! the last time I saw you..."

"Yeah, I know. We got busted in Windsor for knocking off that liquor store," Fred explained.

As they all got reacquainted, Sheila was very quiet, just standing there holding her compact and fixing her face. The four men—Abe, Phil, Fred and Jack—sat down at a large poker table and poured themselves each a large shot of *Log Cabin* bourbon, some of the best bootlegged whiskey in the joint. Within minutes they got down to real mobsterlike business.

As Abe sat under the swinging light, he spoke.

"Listen, you guys, the heat is on," he said. "I talked to Al just a few days ago and he informed me that Chicago is buzzing like a hornet's nest. Feds are cracking down. Too many mobs moving in our territory in Chicago. Scarface wants one mob wiped out," Abe informed the others as they sat and drank.

Abe kept talking to the three mobsters, informing them, "The big man will come up with a hundred Gs if we do a hit job for him."

"What d'we gotta do?" Jack asked.

"Simple!" Abe replied. "Mow down Bugsy and his gang."

Jack asked, "When and where?"

"Valentine's Day, Chicago," Abe replied.

All four men sat quietly for a moment. You could hear the loud banging of the drums below; Krupa was going through his routine with the band.

Phil looked at his boss, Abe, and said, "Count me in."

Both Fred and Jack agreed. "Damn, we can't stand that lousy rat Moran any longer either. Count us in, too."

It was a beautiful set-up. All these guys were first-hand killers with plenty of experience behind them. Fred "Killer" Burke was wanted in Indiana, Ohio, Kentucky and Wisconsin for murders. Phil and his brother Harry were ruthless killers as well. Killing was their business and it didn't bother them in the least, especially with Capone coming up with a hundred grand for the slaughter.

Abe assured the men that all the details of the hit would be arranged and instructions from Capone would be coming soon. After a last minute toast—a slug of old *Log Cabin*—Abe, Sheila and Phil wandered back downstairs to join in the excitement before heading back to the Big Fish Inn.

From the meeting upstairs, this night would make history. Plans came together and the Purple Gang would become part of the St. Valentine's Day Massacre. As for Sheila, she couldn't care less. Her mind was on men and what they could do for her sensuous ways of excitement.

As Krupa was bringing his band to the close of a slow and easy dance, Sheila and Abe were stuck together like glue as they finished dancing on the dimly lighted floor. Sheila's eyes kept moving towards the table at which they had been sitting.

Harry finally came in from outside where he had been watch-dogging and sat down at their table. Phil looked at Harry, and Harry looked at the two dancing. Sheila could sense jealousy from the two Keywell brothers.

As Abe and Sheila danced closely by the two brothers, they became highly excited. She kept pushing her body against Abe.

Finally, when the dance ended, Harry remarked to Phil, "What a doll. What a shape!"

"Knock it off, Harry," said Phil. "Can't you see they're coming over to the table now?"

Harry quickly settled down.

As Abe and Sheila approached, Abe said, "Damn! Let's get out of here before somebody gets my number. I know damn well some of Bugsy's men are around here someplace. I can smell them a mile away."

Abe immediately motioned to Phil, and he in turn jumped up, ran outside to the car and started the engine. The other three made a quick exit and jumped into the Studebaker and sped away. The tires squealed on the wet pavement as the car headed south down the road. Harry grabbed a sawed-off shotgun that was specially mounted on the back side of the front seat. He had noticed a pair of headlights pulling out of the parking lot at the Cat Club.

Cool as a cucumber, Harry said, "Bugsy's rats are following us. I can feel it in my bones."

"Keep a sharp watch on that car," said Abe.

Both Abe and Phil pulled out their .45 automatics at that point.

Abe looked over at Phil, who was driving the car, and said, "Look, Phil, we were spotted by one of Bugsy's men, sure as hell. One of his stooges spotted me and Sheila dancing at the club. Our only chance is to outsmart them. We'll go down the road a couple of miles. Turn off at that old covered bridge at Jordan Junction and wait for them, then, wham! We'll shatter them to pieces with our submachine guns. Okay, Phil?" Abe said.

"Right," Phil replied.

They waited until the car chasing them got close to the bridge. The three Purples quickly stopped their car, jumped out and hid inside by the walls of the bridge. As the other car entered the bridge, they shot the hell out of them. Bam-bam-

bam-bam-bam! Wham! The inside of the bridge lit up like downtown Broadway, and then there was a huge explosion. The car burst into flames as the three Purples scrambled for their car parked on the opposite side of the bridge. The bridge started flaming furiously as they sped away.

"We got 'em! We blasted 'em!" Harry shouted.

"Let's take the back way down to Ellsworth," Abe said, "so nobody will get on our tail."

"Good thinking," Phil said enthusiastically.

It was rainy and dark, and they were assured that they could escape any further problems on their trip back to the inn.

Traveling down the old highway, Phil said, "Abe, I'm sure we got 'em. That'll be two or three less rats in Bugsy's pack."

As the Purples fled down the road, the morning sun was coming up on the eastern horizon. This back route indeed was a very treacherous one. This did not bother Phil or the other two Purples, for they knew this stretch of road like the backs of their hands. Many times, during their escape routes from hijackings, they traveled this back road, thickly wooded, with hairpin curves and little knolls. Hardly a house or a living soul would be sighted on their journey back to the Big Fish Inn.

Sheila, sitting between Phil and Abe, was kind of stunned from the shock of the killings and explosion back at the junction. She kept her mouth shut and started cuddling up to Abe like a little kitten. Abe gave her a gentle kiss on the cheek, figuring that would settle her down. Truthfully, Sheila didn't need any settling down, because she was as tough and cold-blooded as the mob she was riding with.

"Abe, honey," whispered Sheila in his left ear, "I feel good tonight. Let's finish this night off good—I mean real good. When we get back to the hotel, let's have a few drinks on the big sofa by the fireplace."

"Sounds good to me," Abe replied.

At that point, Abe's and Sheila's blood began to warm as their heartbeats intensified. Sheila was ready. Abe knew it.

"Step on it, Phil. We've got to get back in a hurry," Abe demanded.

Harry was still watch-dogging in the back seat.

Abe shouted to Harry, "If you see anything suspicious, holler."

"Got ya," answered Harry.

By now it was becoming daylight. The sun was breaking through the sky, and it appeared that it was going to be a nice day. Sheila felt good as she was sort of daydreaming, looking through the tall pine trees with the sun shining on her tan face. Sheila was dark complected, her father being of Greek-Italian descent.

As the Studebaker kept rolling down the old road, hitting high speed on some of the hairpin curves, Phil had a hard time controlling the car on the wet road.

Abe spoke up. "When we get close to the inn, start slowing down, Phil. We got to be plenty alert. You never can tell, one of Bugsy's rats might have outsmarted us. Look around good when we get to the inn."

All agreed on that, so they cautiously approached the long driveway to the hotel. When they stopped, Sheila slipped out of the car first. Her dress went clear up to her behind. Abe was helping her out the door and couldn't help notice Sheila's beautiful body. He knew what he was in for when they got settled inside. Abe sent Phil and Harry uptown to Ellsworth to do some nosing around. He wanted to know if there might be some unfamiliar faces hanging around town.

George, who had been alertly watching the place all night, was tired and nervous. Abe told him to get some sleep. That left Abe and Sheila alone for quite some time.

The fire was still burning and crackling as Sheila made two dry martinis. Abe loved dry martinis. Sheila handed Abe his drink as he settled in the big sofa. Sheila walked up to the fire and slowly dropped her dress to the floor. Abe's eyes were riveted to Sheila's trim body, her beautiful long hair highlighted down to her small waistline, breasts beautifully large and full. Young and fresh looking, that was Sheila. Abe craved her!

"Come on over here, baby," demanded Abe.

Abe gently pulled Sheila down to him on the big sofa. His hands caressed her entire body and their lips met in a passion of fire. It was time. Abe and Sheila made vigorous love until the dim rays of light became rays of bright sunshine coming through a nearby window.

Two

Bootlegging For Scarface, Al Capone

Detroit River

Abe was sitting under a big tree by the hotel with all his lieutenants nearby. They had been resting and relaxing all day. Abe spoke.

"Listen, you guys, we gotta scram out of here and head back down to Detroit. My brother Ray is waiting for us at Collingwood Manor. Scarface needs some good booze in Chicago. We'll get it tomorrow night across the river at Riverside."

Harry and Phil knew exactly what that meant: confrontation with the city cops (Black Hand Squad) and the federal boys.

Harry said, "Maybe we can plug a few of those bastards tomorrow night."

"Or better yet," Phil added, "maybe a couple sticks of dynamite."

They both laughed and walked towards their car.

As Abe and Sheila bid farewell, Harry and George crawled in the back seat as usual. Phil took the wheel and they spun off down the main highway to Detroit.

They drove for hours, only stopping at a roadside inn for some coffee and a bite to eat. Harry spent most of his time checking over all the guns in the back seat. Abe was trying to catch a few winks of sleep now and then between thinking about his rum-running job coming up shortly.

Finally arriving in Detroit during midday, they greeted Abe's brother, Ray Bernstein, at an alley alongside the Collingwood Manor Apartments, the Purples most recent headquarters. The four men bunked down in the apartment, while Ray slipped out to meet one of Pete Licavoli's boys. The Purples had a truce with the Licavoli mob.

Most all of the illegal liquor from Canada was picked up by the Licavoli mob at Riverside, Ontario, across the river. The mob would sign manifests and take cases of Canadian whiskey and label them for the Bahamas and Nassau. The Canadian officials thought they were shipping the booze from Riverside to Nassau. Mobsters would take a speedboat and run for it across the Detroit River. They had lookouts on Belle Isle, positioned in the trees, with huge flashlights in two colors, red and green. Red meant the federal patrol boats were out; green meant they were docked, go ahead. And then they would dash across the river. Nothing to it. The mobsters had faster speedboats than the feds and police. Usually the police and feds (FBI) worked together to catch the gangsters.

Ray finally got back to the Purples at Collingwood the next morning. Abe was sitting at a small kitchen table, drinking his usual coffee and smoking a cigarette. A bottle of whiskey was within his arm's reach. There was a knock on the apartment door, and Abe quickly pulled out his automatic. His nerves were a little jumpy from his trip the night before. Abe knew it was his brother Ray. He could tell by the knock—two quick ones. Abe put the pistol back in his holster and let Ray inside.

They both sat down, and Ray said, "Abe, it's all set. We show up at Riverside and we get our stuff. Cost me plenty, but Al will pay us plenty, too. It's one of the best shipments they've had in some time."

That evening, the Purples headed over to a fancy Italian restaurant on Clairmont Street. They loathed the Italians in that part of town, but liked their food. The Purples sat down and ordered big plates of spaghetti and bottles of Dago red.

As they sat and dined, chatting with each other, they seemed far apart from everybody else in the restaurant. The time and place was their heyday. Most of the Purples were in their early twenties and had plenty of money to enjoy city nightlife. They wore expensive, conservative suits, mostly blues and grays, and pointed shoes. They weren't known as big drinkers and they behaved themselves when at restaurants and bars. The Purples were never too shabby looking, and their choice of women tended to be teenage showgirls, beautiful and quite quotable. Despite the glamorous image, the Purples were thugs pure and simple. They depended on violence rather than brains to get ahead in the underworld.

During dinner, two young women dressed in fancy apparel came over to the table and joined them for awhile. Ray Bernstein knew both of the girls, because he had slept with both of them off and on. They were showgirls in a downtown club.

Ray spoke to one of the girls. "Shirley, how about you and I takin' in a late show at the Princes?"

"Sure, honey baby," Shirley replied.

"Listen, Ray," Abe said, "you better get back by tomorrow. You know what's up tomorrow night."

Ray responded, "Don't worry, Brother Abe, I'll be back."

They all looked around and cautiously got up from the table, sharply looking left and right for trouble. Anybody looking suspicious might be a member of the Dago mob. They were known to hang out in this area of town. The Purples hated Wops, and the Dagos hated the Purples. Abe pulled out a big roll of bills from his side pocket and laid a big one on the table. They dashed to their car and sped off.

It was late, so they turned in for the night. They slept restlessly, thinking of their task ahead. Morning came and they hurriedly ate some breakfast that Ray's girlfriend was whipping up. Shirley had spent the night with Ray at the apartment.

"How do you like your eggs?" Shirley asked as the gang dressed in the adjoining room.

Sunnyside up seemed to be the popular choice among the Purples. After breakfast, Abe talked over their plans for the night ahead.

"Phil, you drive us down to the dock. Harry and Ray will handle the boats. We'll need two of those big ones that's docked under the roof. George and I will handle the submachine guns [better known as the Chicago typewriters]," Abe explained. "By the way, Ray," Abe continued, "don't forget that box of dynamite."

The night air was chilly. A touch of snow was falling, typical for the early part of February. The river was not frozen over; Detroit had had an early January thaw. Two thugs from Al Capone's gang parked their armored truck close to the dock. They would help transfer the booze from boat to truck, then hightail it out of Detroit to one of Capone's warehouses in Cicero, just outside Chicago.

The Purples took off in their boats, speeding across the river, keeping a sharp eye for the police boats. In a few short minutes they would arrive at Riverside, the Canadian border point. All arrangements for the pickup had been made. Canadian authorities were willing and ready to sell and transfer the liquor to the thugs. Abe slipped the paper manifest to the port authority officer. The hoods quickly loaded the cases of Canadian whiskey in the speedboats. Wasting no time, the Purples took off at full speed, cautiously looking in every direction and most of all toward Belle Isle, where they had lookouts in the trees ready to signal them.

As Harry was navigating one of the big boats at full speed, he spoke to his brother. "Phil, look quick, over toward Belle Isle. Green light flashing."

"Okay, Harry, give this sucker all you got. We gotta make the other side fast!" Phil said.

In the meantime, the Bernstein brothers and George Lewis were trailing Harry and Phil's boat by about twenty-five yards. Abe kept looking towards Belle Isle, because he just didn't trust the way things had been going on the river. Just a few nights back, two speedboats from the Licavoli gang had been nailed for rum-running. Ten gang members had been arrested and two powerboats confiscated by the Black Hand Squad. Abe was taking a final look toward Belle Isle when he saw a red light.

"Son of a bitch!" Abe shouted. "George, hand me a couple sticks of dynamite, quick!"

Both speedboats took a sharp turn to the right. They

headed upriver to evade a police boat that was bearing down on them fast. Abe signaled to Phil's boat to turn out toward shore, while Ray would try to outrun them upstream. Abe ordered Ray to swing the powerboat around and head straight for the police boat. This quick maneuver allowed Abe to toss in a stick of dynamite that would blow them to kingdom come.

As the police boat exploded a few seconds later, the sky lit up from the burning boat. Abe's boat came to a stop.

Abe shouted loudly, "Suckers!"

A few screams were heard from men in the cold water. Abe grinned a little from the corners of his mouth and ordered the boat to proceed. Ray headed the speedboat up the river, while Abe and George looked over their haul of bootlegged liquor. Abe wanted to make sure the boxes of booze were still tied down securely after such a rumpus. About a half mile upstream, they met the Keywell brothers in the other boat. The Purples knew the feds and the cops would be out searching for them, but that didn't matter too much, for Capone's lieutenants had the law officials in Detroit paid off. There was so much corruption in Detroit, as in Chicago and Cleveland, that dirty money changing hands between gangsters and lawmen was a regular practice.

After regrouping, the Purples decided to lie low for awhile in their speedboats in a more heavily populated docking area until the police gave up searching.

As they sat in their boats, Abe said, "One of you guys got a cigarette?"

George threw him a pack of Luckies from across the boat. "Pass 'em around," he said, and then pulled out a silver flask he had tucked in his side vest pocket. "We might as well have a couple snorts. It's going to get pretty damn chilly out here," he suggested.

"Good idea," said Abe as he tipped up the flask and took a big gulp.

They passed the flask around a couple of times and chatted for about an hour or so, talking mostly about women they had made love with. Men seem to talk about things like that when they get together.

Another boat was anchored nearby. It was lit up and loud music could be heard coming from it.

Ray said, "Listen, you guys, I hear music and laughter. Sounds like somebody's having a party on that big boat. It's a cabin cruiser," he added.

"How lucky can we get," said Abe. "It's loaded with women dancin', drinkin' and howlin'. Some old geezer is whooping it up with a bunch of young chicks. Let's crash 'em," Abe continued.

"One of us has to stay here by the boats to keep an eye out," Ray said.

Abe suggested that they go aboard posing as federal agents and pretend to be looking for someone.

As they rushed in on the crowd dancing on the top deck of the cruiser, Abe shouted out, "Put 'em up, this is a raid. We're FBI."

He ordered all of them to stand against a nearby bulkhead.

"Ray, search them from top to bottom," Abe ordered.

Abe did not want to take any chances. They might be carrying concealed weapons. Everything came to a halt. Music stopped on the Victrola. Abe made a switch: Instead of a good time, like they had planned, the Purples would rob this rich bunch of socialites.

Most of the women were half undressed and drunk. The old geezer was a Detroit city judge, about three times older than the young women.

"Phil and Harry," shouted Abe, "take all of them down below and take everything they got."

The women were wearing expensive watches and diamonds and had plenty of cash in their purses. Some of them were so drunk that they tried making love to the gangsters. One was so far gone, she took off her bra and panties and then fell to the floor. The gangsters quickly tied them all up and got out of there fast. When they got back to their boats, they had quite a haul of jewelry and cash.

"Nice going, boys!" Abe said as he sat down in the boat. He lit a cigarette and took a slug of whiskey from George's flask.

Ray said, "Let's get these boats out of here. We've got a lot of whiskey that's got to be trucked out of Detroit by tomorrow morning."

"Right! Let's head down the river. Now!" Abe said in a stern voice.

Phil and Harry took off first, looking cautiously as Abe's boat followed. All the mobsters felt pretty good; their night's work on the river had ended very profitably and without serious trouble.

In a very short time they arrived at their dock. They spotted Capone's truck waiting by the unloading area. Two of Capone's gunmen were anxiously waiting to help load up the bootleg whisky and head for Capone's warehouses near Cicero.

"Hurry!" shouted Abe as the gangsters loaded their contraband on the big stake-body truck.

As Abe was giving orders to the men loading, he said to one of Capone's men, "Listen! You tell Capone that the Keywell brothers and George Lewis will be joining him day after tomorrow in Chicago. Got the message?" Abe insisted.

"I'll tell Capone for sure," said one of the men.

After about half an hour, the mobsters had a good-sized load of bootleg whiskey ready to go. Capone's men didn't want to waste any time getting out of Detroit. They were on their way and speeding toward Chicago by mid-morning.

The Purples headed back to their Collingwood apartment. On the way they stopped at a little speak-easy called Come On In on Woodward Street. It was owned by one of Licavoli's mobsters, Papa John Priziola. He had a bartender named Tiny Sam working there. Tiny Sam weighed about 365 pounds. The Purples used him now and then as a muscle-man to settle union and labor disputes at the Chevy plant. He could crush a man's head between his hands.

As the five Purples walked in the entrance way, Tiny Sam greeted them with a very loud voice.

"Hello, my friends!" he boomed while hammering his huge fist on top of the bar.

The Purples sat down on their bar stools and Sam poured them a big shot of whiskey with a beer chaser. On the house.

Abe finally said, "How you been, you big lug?"

"Fine," replied Tiny. "I just got back from one of those bathhouses over on Oakland. Boy, I feel great. Betty gave me one of those jobs that's out of this world," Tiny Sam continued.

"Tiny, hand me over some of that bologna and cheese," said Abe. "We're starvin'. Been out on the river foolin' around all night," Abe said, rubbing his hands back and forth.

As Tiny Sam handed the Purples a big plate full of meat and cheese, he said, "On the river? I bet I know what you were up to! I heard a big explosion off in that direction, down by the docks, about midnight. Some kind of rumpus—gunfire and sirens screamin'."

"That was us, all right," Abe admitted.

In about an hour, the Purples finished their food and drinks.

Abe looked at Tiny behind the bar and said, "I might need you in a couple days, over by the Bud and Chevy plant. We got some guys that need some roughing up. They're giving the union bosses too much trouble," Abe continued. "I'll let you know when. Stay away from Oakland, you big bum!" Abe said to Tiny as the Purples walked out to their car, laughing.

When they got to their apartment, Shirley was standing by the front entrance, holding a big suitcase.

Ray said, "Shirley, what in the hell is going on?"

"I packed and got out of my place in a hurry," she said. "Some big bastard been trying to mess around with me for weeks. He lives next door. He's a slob and I hate his guts. Even tried raping me right smack in the hallway."

"Don't worry, Shirley baby," said Ray, "I'll take care of that punk before the night's over. Go on upstairs, Shirley. You can stay with me for a while. Okay, fellows?" Ray asked, looking at the rest of the Purples.

"Sure! We don't mind," responded Abe and the gang. "We need someone to take care of our apartment and cook a little anyways," said Abe. "You're a nice girl, Shirley. We all like you like a sister. Isn't that right, boys?"

They all agreed.

That night, after they had a bite to eat, Abe and Ray sat in the kitchen talking and drinking coffee. Ray spoke up.

"I'm going over to Shirley's old apartment and beat the hell out of that rapist pig."

"Cool down," his brother said. "Forget about that now. We got more important things to do. Listen up, you guys," Abe shouted to the rest of the Purples who were playing cards in the nearby living room. "We got some big stuff coming up soon. Harry, Phil and George, you guys are going to drive up to Chicago and meet up with the Capone gang. Remember that meeting with Jack McGurn and Fred Burke at the Cat Club near Charlevoix?"

"Yeah, we remember," said Harry.

"Okay. Get ready. You're on your way day after tomorrow," Abe announced. "Harry knows exactly where to go. Take plenty of fire power. Don't forget!"

Time passed quickly and the three mobsters were on their way—ready to make gangland history and surely not ever really knowing it. A ruthless plan was being constructed by Al Capone to gun down a Chicago mob that would be the bloodiest massacre ever in the history of the underworld.

Three

Purples Assist in St. Valentine's Day Massacre,

Chicago, February 14, 1929

The battle between Al Capone and George Bugs Moran for control of Chicago's North Side reached its peak in 1929. Several of Capone's top lieutenants had been killed by Moran's gunners, while Scarface took a hike to Miami Beach. While at his new home there, Capone decided that drastic measures were called for and ordered Moran's entire gang annihilated. His scheme was diabolically clever and deadly.

On February 13, 1929, George Lewis and Harry and Phil Keywell pulled up and parked in front of the Hawthorne Hotel in Chicago. The Purples had arrived in the Windy City.

"Hurry," said Phil, "we gotta meet Jack and Fred in Capone's office at noon sharp."

As they knocked on a massive, ornate door, it opened and one of Scarface's thugs said, "Come on in, you mugs. Sit down and have a drink."

As the same man poured them a big glass of whiskey, Fred and Jack came in from another room where they had been entertaining a couple of nice looking prostitutes. The office was completely armored and took up the whole third floor.

"Hi, boys," Jack said. "So we meet again! Listen," he insisted, "at about ten o'clock tomorrow morning here at the office, we're going to call Mike O'Banion at his flower shop. Harry, you do the calling. You know the O'Banions. You did business with Mike's old man, Dion, a couple years ago. He'll believe what you tell him," continued Jack. "Have O'Banion call Moran and tell him that a special shipment of bonded whiskey recently hijacked right off the river will be available. He'll bite. I know Moran."

The O'Banions and Moran were closely knitted on the North Side. They trusted each other. Moran was a long-time friend of Mike's father, who had been gunned down by a rival gang. Bugsy would believe O'Banion.

That night of the 13th, the Purples took a room at the Hawthorne and settled in at a secluded lounge in the hotel. They decided to have a few drinks before retiring to their rooms. Before leaving for Florida, Capone left orders to his men to keep the Purples happy while in Chicago. After all, they were doing Scarface a good deed indeed. Before the evening was over, the three Purples were having a good time because Capone's men had ordered three of their top prostitutes to entertain them all through the night.

The next morning the Purples appeared at Al Capone's

office sharply at ten o'clock. Jack McGurn and Fred Burke likewise were there waiting.

A little anxious, Fred asked, "Have a good time last night, boys?"

"Sure did," Harry said. "Where did you get those gals? They were terrific!"

"They're some of Al's hottest girls," Jack explained.

It was getting time to make that call to Mike O'Banion. Jack knew O'Banion would be at the flower shop. Harry Keywell called and told O'Banion about a hijacked load of special bonded whiskey that had just come off the river. O'Banion then called Moran and convinced him to buy the liquor. Moran took the bait, hook, line and sinker. He ordered his truck to go over to his garage on the North Side. Moran said he would be there in a half hour.

Mike O'Banion immediately called back Harry Keywell and said Moran and his gang would be at the garage in a half hour. It was a set-up, but O'Banion would not know any differently. He thought Harry was doing him a favor.

Jack spoke, "Listen up you guys! We're going to surprise 'em at Moran's garage on Clark Street. We'll drive over there in our black Cadillac, dressed in police uniforms, pretending we're making a police raid. Grab those police uniforms piled up over there on the big chair and pass them around," Jack demanded. "We'll leave in a couple of minutes."

Jack paused a second while slipping the police uniform on. "One thing for sure, men," looking at the four other gangsters dressing. "Mow these characters down and nobody stays alive. I mean nobody! Shoot to kill!" ordered Jack Machine Gun McGurn. "That's the way Capone wants it. Got it?" Jack continued.

"Got it!" replied the men. "No mercy for nobody."

The five gangsters went down the back stairway of the hotel and hopped into one of Capone's armored black Cadillacs that had been parked at the rear of the building. Nobody saw them drive away.

Jack said, "Toss me one of those machine guns. Make sure all your guns are loaded up to full capacity," he said to all the thugs. "We're gonna mow down all of those bastards. Every last one of them!" Jack shouted.

In about fifteen minutes, their black Cadillac rounded a corner where they could see the garage. A big sign placed in the front window read S.M.C. Cartridge Company. It was owned by one of Moran's flunkies. Waiting inside were six of Bugsy's gang. One member did not belong to the Moran gang. A total of seven men—bootlegger Adam Heyes; Moran's top gunners, the deadly brothers Frank and Pete Gusenberg; John May, a safe-blower; speak-easy owner Al Weinshank; bank robber James Clark; and Dr. Reinhardt H. Schwimmer, an optometrist fascinated by gangsters—lounged about on the premises. A German shepherd named Highball, scampered about the trucks and cars parked in the garage. The men waited impatiently for Moran to arrive, but he stopped at a candy store just up the street, half a block away, to buy a pack of cigarettes. While in the candy store, Moran saw the black Cadillac roll up to the curb and stop in front of the garage. Five men dressed as policemen went inside. Moran waited, figuring it was a pinch and would eventually scram out of the candy store and escape.

Neighbors in adjoining buildings then heard what they later described to police as pneumatic drills. The police emerged minutes later with two men, apparently under arrest. The squad car drove off leisurely (the squad car, Capone's men and the Purples). The dog began to howl.

The landlady in the next building was disturbed by the

dog's whining and sent one of her roomers to the garage to investigate. He came outside two minutes later, his mouth gaping, his face ash color. He ran up the stairs to tell his landlady, "The place is full of dead men."

The policemen entering the garage stepped back in shock at the sight. It was obvious to police that seven men had been lined up against the north brick wall of the building and machine-gunned while their backs had been turned. Each man had big rolls of cash on them—Heyes, $1,135; Weinshank, $1,200...Capone's killers had not bothered to rummage through their victims' pockets.

One man survived the slaughter for a few hours. Frank Gusenberg died in a hospital nearby. His brother Pete had died kneeling, slumped against a chair where James Clark had fallen on his face with half his head blown off. Heyes, Schwimmer, Weinshank, and May sprawled lifeless on their backs, their brains spilling onto the greasy garage floor.

Moran exploded when he heard of the almost total destruction of his gang. When police asked him who the caller was who set up the gang, he raved like a madman. While Frank Gusenberg, in the hospital during his dying moments, staunchly upheld the underworld's code of silence, Moran did not. Pressured by the news media for a comment, Moran blurted out: "Only Capone kills like that."

The St. Valentine's Day Massacre marked the end of any significant gangland opposition to Capone in Chicago. He could now control the rackets without gangland interference. The feds had been pushing for the Militia to come in the city of Chicago and settle the gangland wars. Now that Moran's gang was gone, Scarface could roam about in his armored limousines without fear of any dominant force like the state militia.

Later that day, the five gangsters who had pulled off the biggest gangland massacre in all time leisurely drove away in a big black Cadillac, headed out of town on the north-bound highway toward Charlevoix, Michigan. Destination, the Big Fish Inn, the Purple Gang's famous hideout. The Chicago police had widespread stakeouts throughout the suburbs; however, the thugs cautiously slipped through them as they sped off quickly toward the north.

Four

Purple's Speak-Easy, The Blue Devil

Near the waterfront,
Miami, Florida.

The killers, Jack Machine Gun McGurn, Fred Killer Burke, George Lewis, and brothers Harry and Phil Keywell, were now speeding up to the Big Fish Inn. Abe and Ray Bernstein were getting ready to fly down to Miami to buy into some night clubs and brothels around the outskirts of the city. Al Capone and Lucky Luciano were going to give the Bernstein brothers a piece of their pie in gambling and prostitution. It was a gesture of brotherly love, Mafia style. But if the real reason were to be known: fear, not love. Capone and Luciano feared for their lives from the ruthless Purples.

While Abe and Ray Bernstein were taking a taxi over to the Detroit Airport on Maple Street a little after midnight, a light drizzle falling outside, newspaper boys were out on the streets of Detroit yelling, "Extra! Extra! Read all about it. Valentine's Day Massacre. Extra! Extra! Valentine's Day Murders! Gangland Massacre! Extra! Extra!"

Abe quickly ordered the taxi to pull over! "I gotta buy a paper." Abe stepped out of the taxi and whistled to a newsboy. "Over here, over here!" Abe shouted. Back in the taxi, Abe started reading the front page.

"Ray," he said real quick to his brother sitting beside him. "They got 'em, they got 'em. They mowed the bastards down. Got every damn one of them," Abe continued. "They got away too! They skipped out of town, Ray. You know where they went? Don't ya, Ray?" Abe said.

"Sure! Up to the Big Fish Inn."

"Right. They're safe! They're hiding out up there. I always told them that when things got hot, high tail it for the Big Fish."

As their taxi pulled up close to the tri-motor transport, they could hear the big engines warming up. Abe, smiling, handed the taxi driver a five spot and said, "Keep the change, buddy. Have a nice day." Abe, at times, was a gentleman and could be very nice and warm-hearted to certain souls. On the other hand, he could be cold, ruthless and a brutal killer.

The transport plane belonged to Al Capone. He used it privately for transporting friends and personal cargo (mostly illegal contraband) between Chicago and Miami. Capone's taste for comfort and luxury surely showed in his airplane. The front half of the fuselage had been converted into, you might say, a first class hotel suite, a lounge bar with big plushy sofas and a small kitchenette for snacks.

As the Bernstein brothers stepped into the armored airplane, they noticed four young women sitting toward the front of the plane. They were prostitutes being transferred from Chicago down to a new pleasure palace outside Miami Beach.

While Abe was relaxing in his seat, his brother Ray was becoming quite nervous, for he didn't like flying in airplanes. Airline travel was a fairly new type of transportation, and Abe and Ray had not become too familiar with flying.

"Fasten your seatbelts. We will be taking off in just a few minutes," said the pilot on the intercom. After a few moments, the pilot spoke again, "No smoking for ten minutes. Thank you."

Abe put his head back against the head cushion and started to doze off. It wasn't long before he was thinking about Harry, Phil and George probably nestled down by now at the Big Fish Inn. He knew Sheila would be there and thought about her and the rest of the Purples. Abe was anxious to hear more about the killings at Moran's hangout on North Clark Street. Soon as they got to Miami they would find out more about it from Capone's headquarters in Miami Beach.

They flew for about three and a half hours before they set down at a little airport outside Atlanta, Georgia. They needed to refuel the plane.

A couple of Capone's men who were escorting the prostitutes on the plane went back to the baggage section and carried out onto the airstrip a couple of good-sized packages. While the plane was being refueled, some hoody looking men drove up to the plane and transferred the packages to their big limousine.

The pilot gave orders over the intercom that nobody was

to leave the plane. Abe looked out the passenger side window in the dim light. Two of Capone's men were talking with the men in the limousine. They were waving their hands around. Suddenly the limousine drove off.

One of the young prostitutes motioned to Abe to come on back to the lounge. Abe poked Ray in the side and said, "Come on, Ray, wake up! We got some chicks that want us to join them for a little party. Come on!" Abe insisted.

As Abe and Ray sat down near the bar in big, soft padded chairs, one of the girls said, "Where are you gentlemen from? Chicago?"

"No," said Abe, "we're from Detroit."

As one of the young girls poured some drinks, she said, "My name is Toots. You guys look like you need a drink." She handed Abe and Ray two fancy glasses of champagne. Toots introduced the other girls and, likewise, Abe introduced Ray.

In about a half hour, as the Bernstein brothers and the prostitutes were indulging in laughter and drinking, they could hear the engines starting up. At that moment, the pilot made an announcement to fasten seat belts and not to smoke for ten minutes. He informed the passengers they would be landing in Miami, Florida, hopefully in about two hours, without any bad weather predicted.

The two Purples were becoming well acquainted with the prostitutes by now. As moments passed by, Abe and Ray were beginning to feel more relaxed. Ray started making passes at the women. It was not long before the women were hugging and kissing the two brothers while, in turn, Abe and Ray were trying to slip some of their clothing off. It wasn't long before the two girls had nothing more than bras and panties on.

Suddenly the aircraft dropped in altitude, and the party

came to an abrupt end. When the plane straightened out, everybody was a little shaken up and they settled down to more normal conditions.

Finally, sitting back in his big chair, Abe said, "What in the hell happened?"

One of the girls said, "We hit an air pocket. It'll shake you up a little. I've flown down here by the coast before. It's like that down here in Florida," the girl explained.

Finally the pilot said over the intercom, "Stay in your seats and buckle down. We're getting into some bad weather. We'll be landing in a short time, so please stay calm. Everything will be fine. Thank you."

The remaining flight was rough and after landing, the passengers were feeling a little bewildered. Darkness was still lingering when a big Cadillac pulled up to the plane. Then two smaller cars pulled up behind the big Cadillac. As the two Purples stepped out of the plane, Abe noticed Scarface in the back seat of the Caddy. One of Capone's thugs hopped out of the vehicle and opened the rear door. Capone stepped out, and quickly three of his men holding machine guns surrounded the area.

Scarface reached out and hugged Abe and Ray. Capone spoke, "Welcome! Welcome to the sunny state of Florida. Gentlemen, get in the car and we will be on our way to my home. I want you to meet Lucky Luciano and some of his boys. You haven't met him yet. He's my guest. He's staying for a while. You'll like Luciano."

The prostitutes climbed in one of the other mobster's car and they all sped off. As they traveled down the highway towards Miami Beach, Scarface said, "Boys, it's done. The Morans and O'Banions are finished. They mowed them to pieces, according to the newspapers down here."

"We're going to, I mean, Lucky and I, are going to pay

you guys back for that job up in Chicago yesterday," Capone continued. "Lucky and I have quite a few clubs and whores working for us here in Miami. We got too much business. We need help, so how about you and brother Ray taking some of the load off our hands. What ya say, Abe?" Capone said. "We'll sell you a club over on the strip by the beach. How does that sound?" insisted Capone.

"You Purples did me one hell of a big favor and I'm not going to forget it," Scarface continued. "There's a little club down by the ship docks. It's a real money maker. You guys will get rich. Real rich! More money in a month than you could make in a year back at Detroit. Those two clubs alone take in about 25 gees a week."

Abe and Ray seemed happy about the night spots that Capone was explaining to them, but they also had other things on their mind. As the limousine was speeding down the highway, they put the window down in the back seat and were enjoying the beautiful sunrise on the expanding ocean to their left, palm trees gently swaying on the nearby shores.

The Purples had just entered into a world that they never had experienced before—big-time crime in a tropical paradise.

The mobsters' cars entered a private drive that wound around a big garden with Spanish moss hanging from big trees. The Purples could see many of Capone's men, tommy guns in hand, scattered here and there around the grounds.

As the gangsters' cars pulled up in front of the rich looking home that Scarface had just recently built, a butler came out and helped Abe and Ray with their small suitcases. They traveled light and if they needed anything on the spur of the moment, they would buy it. The Purples always had big rolls of money in their pockets.

After the Bernstein brothers got settled in their plush bedrooms upstairs, they went to Capone's gigantic outside pool near the rear of the building. The pool was a beautiful work of art made of fancy Tennessee sandstone, with water as blue as the sky, surrounded by huge tropical flowers and plants. Luciano was swimming in the pool along with three beautiful girls. The women were permanent property of Scarface's estate. They lived there. Luciano stepped out of the pool and casually walked over to a nearby breakfast table—looking straight at the Bernstein brothers.

Capone had changed clothing and appeared on the scene. He said, "I want you to meet the one and only, Mr. Lucky Luciano."

The Purples did not show a lot of emotion and shook his hand.

"Sit down, gentlemen," said Luciano. "Have some hot breakfast. You fellows must be hungry after a long flight."

"Sit down. Relax, enjoy, eat," the kingpin insisted.

All four of the mobsters sat down and, while eating, they talked in detail about the massacre up north in Chicago. Capone picked up a morning newspaper that was lying on the top of the breakfast table and shouted out, "Look here. Right on the front page. Says 400 gangsters killed in gang wars alone in Chicago in the last few years. Only two of the murders were solved."

"A real goddamn crazy place," said Lucky Luciano. "Nobody's safe on the streets."

Abe was concerned about his men. He talked to Scarface for a long time as he knew Capone had held telephone conversations with his thugs earlier in the morning at the Hawthorne Hotel, Capone's headquarters. Abe seemed satisfied that his partners had gotten out of Chicago just in time, escaping up to the Big Fish Inn.

In the meantime, the women were splashing around in the pool having a big time.

Capone said, "After you finish eating, take a dip in the pool. My women will teach you boys how to swim." Capone winked and said, "I promise!"

Taking their clothes off down to just undershorts, Abe and Ray jumped in the pool. This was not unusual for poolside activity at Scarface's estate. This was considered fun and exciting by the mobster.

Abe and Ray considered this type of activity just plain stupid. But they were guests of Al Capone's world, so they made the best of it. The Purples were a different breed. They had grown up in a poor, rough-and-tough, dog-eat-dog Jewish neighborhood in Detroit. Now they were learning how big-time crime and corruption would change their way of living.

It wasn't until around noon that Abe and Ray left the pool. They seemed relaxed and ready to conquer the world. They hurriedly dressed in their rooms, for Lucky Luciano wanted to give them a tour of Miami and a perspective view of how people were spending money like water in clubs and brothels around the Miami area. Miami was becoming wild. Thousands of speak-easies and Blind Pigs were popping up all over the city. People were drinking illegal booze and gambling. The city was going crazy. Miami was becoming the nation's leading resort city. From a mangrove swamp, the city was quickly becoming a year-round playground, where the gentle tradewinds gave the city a winter-warm, summer-cool climate only duplicated in a few other small regions of the world. Besides its affable climate, the Miami area possessed a sub-tropical beauty not found elsewhere in the continental United States.

The Bernsteins met Luciano down by Capone's garage area. Luciano said, "Hop in, fellows. I'm driving. We have a lot of territory to cover today."

The three gangsters sped off and soon crossed over Biscayne Bay on a causeway and turned left on Biscayne Boulevard. As Luciano was steering the vehicle, he said, “There’s a little speak-easy over on Ninth Street called the Blue Devil.” Luciano continued, “It’s a real jivey joint, close to the waterfront and the docks. It jumps all night long. Sailors come off their ships down there and give us all kinds of business. They’ve been out to sea for a long time and when they come ashore, they’re hurting for women and a good time.”

“Sounds good!” said Abe, the leader of the Purple Gang. “A spot like that could be very profitable,” he continued.

“It is,” said Luciano. “Twenty gees a week. I’ve got an older prostitute running the place. Her name is Flo. She’s got some of the best whores in town working for her. Those sailors flock in there all night long,” continued Luciano. “We’ll be there in a few minutes,” said Luciano as he continued driving.

As Luciano turned a corner, the Purples spotted the joint. It was situated in a cluster of other buildings on a street lined with swaying palm trees. As the three mobsters got out of their blue roadster, a warm tropical breeze was blowing in from the Bay. Abe and Ray were beginning to enjoy this place called the Playland of America.

A big Navy ship had just recently anchored at one of the piers off Ninth Street, and sailors were going in and out of the Blue Devil left and right as the three mobsters fought their way through the front door.

Once inside, a tall woman with blonde hair came rushing up to Luciano and the two hugged and kissed.

“Lucky! You handsome devil. I haven’t seen you since Christmas. You look great. Give me another hug. I love ya,” the woman said. “Made lots of money for you since the last time you were here, sugar baby. Those Navy ships just keep sailin' in down at the pier," she continued. "Come on upstairs to my suite. We'll have a little drink or two," she insisted.

"Okay," said Luciano. "I got some boys I want you to meet. They're some real good friends of Al and I from up at Detroit. They'll be running this place from now on, babe. They're good guys and they love blondes," Luciano said with a big smile, winking his eye at Abe and Ray.

Finally, Luciano introduced the Purples to the big blonde woman. They sat down by a glass-topped table and started drinking some good bourbon she had nearby.

The three mobsters and Big Flo (as she was known by most people) were casually sitting and having some serious conversation when a buzzer sounded off in her suite. It was an emergency signal that would alarm her of trouble downstairs.

Sure enough, there was a fight going on between some civilians and a couple of Navy petty officers. It was the usual type of brawl over some dumb broad.

The three mobsters and Big Flo rushed downstairs. Bodies were flying left and right. The fact that this speakeasy was a Navy hot spot for sailors made civilians the bad guys. Abe and Ray jumped in and tried to settle things. It seemed the sailors were getting the worst part of the battle. Abe grabbed one of the mean guys around the waist from behind, and his brother Ray punched the brute right smack in the stomach. The big brute fell to the deck.

The other guy was coming down on Abe with a big chair. Abe swiftly turned around and gave a ferocious right to the guy's jaw. Blood was dripping all around as the two Bernstein brothers picked up the two bodies and threw them out on the street.

The crowd inside was jumping up and down, raving and

yelling. The two brothers quickly became heroes. Abe and Ray came back inside the club and people started shaking their hands.

"Set 'em up, Harry! Drinks on the house," said Flo, standing by the bar. "We got new owners of this place. Abe and Ray Bernstein. They'll take care of you," insisted Flo.

Everybody drank and got back to normal again. The band started playing and people started dancing.

Luciano and Flo went up to her suite while the Purples stayed around the bar and started mingling with the patrons. It was time to show good ownership and friendliness toward their customers. This would be the Purples' new home, at least for now. They would make this spot their headquarters while in Florida.

Eventually Abe and Ray went back upstairs to the suite where Luciano and Big Flo were lounging around.

All three mobsters, after some serious convincing, talked Big Flo into staying on at the Blue Devil. She would be their manager and most trusted person while in Miami.

In a few days, the Purples would move into some empty rooms next to Flo's suite. Flo had worked her way up from the slums of Miami to where she was now. That was quite a deed for her time. She was only thirty years old. Started at prostitution when she was fifteen. Been arrested many times in the Miami red light districts, but always seemed to be able to get out of her jams.

Flo was considered a nymphomaniac by her close friends. The fact that the Bernstein brothers were going to live next door suited Flo with a passion of excitement. Sooner or later Flo would be homing in on her prey. Flo had all the opportunities to have any man whenever she wanted one, with all the men coming in the Blue Devil, but she loved the idea of two men living next door to her.

After spending a good part of the day at the Blue Devil, Luciano and the two Purples finally left and headed for other places.

It was a warm and beautiful day in Miami as the trio drove south down Biscayne Boulevard. Luciano wanted to show the Purples where Capone's warehouse was located. Capone had a whole building loaded with imported illegal rum from Cuba that he was getting ready to unload throughout the city.

Scarface was setting himself up for future plans in Miami. He had a gut feeling that Chicago was getting too hot with the FBI and other small hoods causing too many problems. Capone had been hearing about a small group of FBI agents called the Untouchables formed by Eliot Ness. Capone had an urgency to understand Ness and learn what he could about the Untouchables. Capone felt a personal drive toward Ness that would eventually lead Scarface to ultimate destruction.

Ness, the son of a wholesale baker, was raised with loving strictness by his Norwegian-born parents. From them he learned an appreciation of Shakespeare and the opera.

Ness was an outstanding tennis player while at the University of Chicago. This quiet man with a firm, deep voice majored in commerce and business administration. But since Sherlock Holmes refused to make way in the mind of Eliot Ness for the world of finance, in his spare time and feeling a mild guilt for the hours stolen from his studies, Ness took a jujitsu course and became an expert shot at the Chicago police pistol range.

The lure of detective work was too strong to withstand, and when he was graduated from the University of Chicago in 1925, the humdrum of the business world lost out to the prospect of adventure and excitement.

For two years, Ness had to be content with a post as an investigator for a large insurance company. There was little action and much pavement-pounding as he checked credit ratings and investigated insurance claims. Yet it was solid training which qualified him finally for a post with the United States Department of Justice in the Prohibition Bureau.

But Ness soon learned that Prohibition convictions in a city as wet as Chicago spelled only one thing: bribery. His indignation developed into icy anger and an unshakable determination to do something about it. Capone was his main target.

Eliot Ness laid his plans carefully, and it wasn't long before he was able to put them in operation. Only a small, tightly knit group of agents hand-picked by him would be able to loosen Capone's grip on the law. A group of ten who literally broke the pay-off power of Scarface Al Capone; ten who proved themselves beyond bribery or bullets; ten who became known to the underworld as The Untouchables!

As Ness was beginning his great efforts to stamp out the gangsters of Chicago, the Purples, Scarface Capone and Charles Lucky Luciano were becoming star hoodlums in the playland city of America, Miami.

Five

Capone's Big Party Raided By Cuban Gang

After a long day of business and sightseeing, the Purples and Luciano headed back to Capone's estate at Miami Beach.

As Luciano was driving across the main causeway into Miami Beach, he asked, "What d'ya think about the Blue Devil?"

Abe answered, "Not bad! Not bad at all! I like the Blue Devil."

Then Luciano turned to Ray and said, "What's your opinion?"

"Sounds good! Great club!" answered Abe's brother.

"Fine," said Luciano, "I'll draw up some papers that you boys can sign tomorrow."

"Excellent!" said Abe, the leader of the Purples.

"You and your brother Ray can move in at the Blue Devil tonight, if you like. I'm sure Flo will be looking for you two gentlemen," Luciano said with a big smile on his face.

Luciano parked the car in the parking lot and the three mobsters got out. As Abe was walking up to the side entrance of the estate, he said, "Ray, we've got to call the Big Fish Inn. We gotta find out about our boys. We're the Purples and we stick together."

As the two brothers walked up a huge, padded spiral staircase that led to their rooms, Ray remarked, "Better believe it—we're the Purples! We're the greatest! We're the meanest!"

As soon as they entered their room, Abe grabbed a phone that was sitting on a nightstand by his bed. He quickly dialed a number on the phone. Suddenly, a woman's voice said, "This is the operator."

"Ellsworth, Michigan, 8-2-1-1," Abe replied.

"Thank you," said the operator. "Wait a few minutes for your call."

Abe lit a cigarette and waited patiently for his call to go through. He was thinking as he waited: "Maybe something went wrong. Cops might have got them or something went wrong." Abe was restless.

Finally, a voice on the receiver said, "Hello." Abe recognized the voice immediately.

"Sheila, baby! How's my sweetheart?" Abe asked.

"Fine, honey!" Sheila insisted.

"How are the boys?" Abe asked.

Sheila replied, "They got here a couple days ago.

George Lewis said that on the way up, just outside Muskegon, they ran a police car off the road and it burned and exploded."

"Good, baby," said Abe. "Let me talk to Harry."

"Hi, Abe!" boomed Harry into the phone. "We did 'em in, Abe. Five of us on the hit at the garage on Clark Street: Jack McGurn, Fred Burke, George, my brother Phil and myself. Just like we planned up at the Cat Club in Charlevoix," explained Harry. "We surprised the hell out of them. Mowed them down like sitting ducks. That bastard Bugsy wasn't there. We'll take him down one of these days," insisted Harry.

"Good work, Harry," said Abe.

After Abe chatted awhile with his fellow mobsters, he talked to Sheila again and told her to take good care of his men. Abe said good-bye and placed the receiver in the cradle.

The next day, Abe and Ray Bernstein moved into their new location at the Blue Devil. They needed transportation. Scarface gave them the name of a slick dealing car salesman with whom he had done business. That afternoon they sported a fancy new Cadillac Coupe.

The Bernstein brothers were reaching a new plateau in their lives. They were beginning to enjoy some better things in life aside from killing, robbery and bootlegging.

That day they decided to go to the pony tracks nearby. Although they themselves never had been to a race track, they understood the betting. They had bookies working for them back in Detroit. They asked Flo to go along. Flo loved the ponies and was more than ready to go.

"Bring lots of money," Abe told her.

The two Bernsteins and Flo hopped in their newly purchased Caddy and headed for Hialeah, a little suburb outside Miami. It was a beautiful day and the track would be fast.

As their shiny new Cadillac pulled into the track parking lot, a big black man smoking a large cigar at the main entrance said, "A buck, one dollar to park, please," he insisted as Abe handed him a five spot, saying, "Keep the change, buddy."

"Thank you, sir!"

"Thank you," said the excited man.

After parking their car, the two brothers and Flo walked up to the entrance of a beautiful place called Hialeah Race Park, a wonderful looking structure with a big grandstand. White sand covered the track, with hundreds of palm trees and a beautiful blue lake in the center of the oval. Once inside they chose a nice spot to view the races, close to a fence where they could stand and be next to the excitement.

Flo was starting to feel more comfortable with her new bosses. Her sexual desire for the two brothers was building. Out on the town with two good-looking men, Flo was beginning to make her sensuous moves. She could hardly contain herself. She was happy as a lark.

The second race was just beginning. Flo had gotten to know some of the jockeys pretty well from their visits to the Blue Devil every so often. In fact, Flo got to know everybody well in her little circle of life.

All three quickly looked over their program sheets, and Flo suggested she would run back to the betting booth and place their bets. The horses had already made their appearance in front of the grandstand. The five-minute signal could be heard from the post horn. The ponies would be racing around the track very shortly. Flo had to hurry. She got to the betting booth just in time.

Abe had given Flo a hundred to bet on number 2 that he

had picked. Abe liked the horses that brought up their front feet the highest while parading in front of the grandstand. Number 2 was a long shot, twenty-five to one. The rest of the threesome bet on more of the favorites that had lower odds. As Flo got back to the fence, the horses' gates crashed open.

"They're off and running," came a loud voice from the track's P.A. system.

Abe's horse, number 2, had a good start for the six furlong race. Ray had number 8, and Flo had number 1. As the horses were heading for the halfway mark, Ray's horse, number 8, was in the lead by two lengths. Flo's horse was only a couple horses back from Ray's. Abe's horse was trailing the pack.

Suddenly, the announcer said, "As the horses make their turn for the home stretch, it's Choice Dish in front by a full length. Number 6, Fast Pitch,' coming up from behind. Bobby's Knight, number 1, coming strong. Here they come down the stretch. It's Bobby's Knight, number 1, in front by a half length; number 5, Big Boy, right behind. It's Bobby's Knight the winner, second is Big Boy, third is number 6, Fast Pitch, and coming in fourth is number 2, Too Late."

Flo was jumping up and down as she shouted, "I'm a winner! I'm a winner!"

Abe grabbed her around her waist and picked her up as he said, "You lucky doll. You can buy us dinner tonight."

"Sure will," agreed Flo. "We'll stop at that Chinese restaurant on the way back to the Blue Devil," she insisted.

After a few more races, the Bernstein brothers and Flo had had enough. It was starting to rain in sunny Florida as the trio headed for their car. Heavy rain started falling as they got into the car. There were big flashes of lightning and thunder was banging as they drove off and headed for Miami.

Rain was coming down like cats and dogs. Abe had the windshield wipers on full speed. He had to make a left turn to get on 11th Street and then straight down 11th to Chin-Wa-Lo, a Chinese restaurant not too far from the Blue Devil.

When Abe pulled up to the curb by the restaurant, the rain was still falling. As a flash of lightning lit the sky, they ran hurriedly to the entrance.

As the three walked into the restaurant, they thought they were in China. Once inside, the surroundings and environment were completely Chinese. Oriental flowers and gardens throughout the restaurant. In the center of the dining area was a big waterfall and pool surrounded by beautiful colored rocks. Chinese music was to be heard as they sat down to order.

Flo read the menu for the two brothers, for she could read Chinese a little. All three of them ordered chow mein dinners with egg rolls. While they were eating, two Chinese dancers were moving about from table to table. Flo was quite impressed with it all, but Abe and Ray didn't know what to make of it. They were not familiar with such places as Chinese restaurants. The Purples were more acquainted with the rough and tough bar scene, like "a shot and a beer chaser."

After dinner, the Purples and Flo walked down the street to where their car was parked. All three were holding on to each other with Flo in the middle. Flo spoke.

"Gentlemen, thank you so much for an enjoyable day. Tonight, I will return the favor. I'm sure you boys will enjoy what I have in store for you!"

"Golly, Flo, what d'ya mean by that?" asked Abe.

"Yeah, Flo, what do you mean?" asked Ray.

"Honey buns! Just wait and see," Flo said convincingly as she stepped into the car.

That got the two brothers' brains stirred up a little, as Abe whispered to Ray, "Ray, I think I know what she's talking about and it ain't tidily-winks. She's out to have a good time tonight in bed. I can see it in her eyes. That's good. We'll take her on, you and I. We'll both give it to her—wham, bam!"

"She's a nympho," Abe whispered to Ray. "Nymphos need a lot of guys to satisfy them, you know," he continued.

"Yeah, I heard that one time," admitted Ray.

The two Purples finally got in their car and headed for the Blue Devil just down the street. When they arrived, the Blue Devil was buzzing with activity. Many Navy vessels were anchored at the piers down by the waterfront. The United States Navy was having war games out in the Atlantic Ocean and in the Caribbean. That was good news for the Miami area. Lots of business. Not only tourist business for the local stores and night spots, but also for the benefit of the underworld activities such as gambling, prostitution and drinking holes.

The Blue Devil was one of those spots to be benefited, located nice and handy for the sailors and officers coming off the big ships docked at the piers. The Bernsteins knew this and would cash in on plenty of dough before they decided to leave for their home grounds in Detroit.

After arriving at their new establishment, the Bernstein brothers had a few drinks with some sailors at the bar and then went up to their rooms to catch a wink or two.

Flo had a good many prostitutes working for her at the Blue Devil. She screened every last one herself before they went to work for her. That way she could get a little pleasure herself, being the nymphomaniac she was.

Prostitutes were roaming all around the place, downstairs as well as upstairs. Abe and Ray didn't seem to mind, though. They were tired, placed their do not disturb sign on the doorknob, and hit the sack. The only thought in their minds was that later in the night they would get a knock on the door from Flo.

Flo was busy talking and socializing downstairs in her little world of fast women and sailors ready to buy sex. Everybody liked Flo. She was full of fun, jolly, always smiling and loved to be around men, most of the time. Sexually seducing and overpowering men was Flo's way of life.

Flo was a big woman, but very well built. Blonde, short hair, blue eyes and light complexion. Over six feet tall, about 165 pounds and 30 years old. She came from a poor section of Miami, from parents exiled from Norway. Her father was a hard-drinking Norwegian fisherman who got into political problems and was smuggled into the United States by a contraband ship that landed in Miami 30 years ago. Flo was born in the slum area of Miami. She worked her way out of the lower parts of the south side fishing wharves to the brothels of Miami Beach.

Flo was hard, but very provocative in her business of sexual fulfillment of men of all ages. She became one of the most talked-about prostitutes in the Miami area. Flo was known to be a hot cookie. That she was! Flo would soon prove this to her newly acclaimed bosses at the Blue Devil, Abe and Ray Bernstein.

It was getting late and Flo ordered the hired hands to close the club for the night. After the Blue Devil was closed good and tight, Flo sat quietly on a bar stool and lit a cigarette while finishing a last drink. A small glimmer of light was shining through a crack in the kitchen door. She inhaled on her cigarette and started to think back to when she was a child of about fifteen, playing around the fishing wharves and helping her dad with the fish nets. On all the other boats, boys helped their fathers with the nets, and sometimes the older boys would grab her and take her inside an old warehouse and hold her down while they fondled and eventually raped her. Strange as it was, that didn't seem to bother her; she seemed to enjoy it.

Suddenly, Flo heard a loud noise at the rear door of the kitchen. The noise brought Flo back to reality. She went into the kitchen, looked outside and saw a dog running down the back alley. The dog must have hit the back door with its paw as it was digging around in some garbage that was lying close to the door. Flo turned the kitchen light off and went upstairs.

Flo walked to Abe and Ray's room, where they were sleeping, and quietly opened their door just a crack so she could peek in. A small, dim light was glowing from a nightstand by Abe's bed. Quickly, Flo went to her room and slipped into a very short negligee. As the silky garment slowly slid down over her large, full breasts and tall body, she quivered and felt a tingle go down her spine. Flo was feeling the excitement of a woman's crowning glory, the sex act; a beautiful gift she could give and receive. Flo picked up a bottle of perfume that was on her dresser and sprayed her entire body as she looked into the mirror and said to herself, "Showtime."

Flo walked over to the Bernstein brothers' room and quietly slipped inside. At that moment, Abe and Ray awoke and were looking right at Flo standing there. She immediately dropped her negligee to the floor and stood naked. The brothers looked at Flo with intensity. Abe and Ray were not surprised at all. In fact, they were waiting for this to happen.

Abe spoke up, "Wow-ee! You look beautiful! Come on over here, baby. You're just what we're lookin' for."

Ray in the meantime said, “Yeah! You look hot, baby!”

It appeared all three were in a very sensual mood.

Flo walked over to their beds and sat down beside Abe. Immediately both kissed each other on the lips and started stroking one another.

As Flo lay back on a big fluffy pillow, she said, “Ray, honey, lay down here.” She motioned him to her side. They fell back on the bed and she started kissing him frantically all over his body.

It wasn’t long before the three were engaged in ultimate forms of sexual activity. They made love for at least an hour.

Ray was beginning to tire somewhat, so he got up and poured himself a drink from a nearby liquor stand. His brother Abe was still going strong with Flo in various acts of lovemaking.

Finally the orgy came to an end, and all three decided to carry on this matter at a later date.

Flo, a little tired but feeling satisfied, went back to her room, showered and went to bed.

In the meantime back in the brothers’ room, Abe spoke: “God! What a woman! She could take care of a dozen all at the same time.”

“You know it, Ray!” Abe said to his brother.

“Yeah, she’s something else,” Ray admitted. “She could go on for ever and ever,” assumed Ray.

“Flo can wake me up any night,” Abe said. “Any night of the week.”

After a good night’s rest, the brothers went downstairs and had breakfast with Scarface and Flo. Capone had dropped by the Blue Devil to talk to the Purples. He had papers for Abe and Ray to sign, and he invited them all over to his estate for a big party he was having on Saturday night. He asked Flo to bring some of her girls over for entertainment.

Scarface had been married for about four years, but he always kept his family at home in Chicago. He never mixed his family with his business. Capone had invited a lot of prominent people for his party, mainly big time judges, city officials and lawmen—a social event to make friends with the elite and high ranks of Miami. After all, it was the Prohibition Era and Capone was setting himself up for millions and millions of dollars to be taken in the Miami area alone. Gambling, bootlegging and prostitution.

Capone had come a long way in his big-time crime world. He had wiped out his rival mobster gang in Chicago, the Moran gang. Now he had one last big event to take care of in Atlantic City. He had summoned most of the big rival mobsters from east of the Mississippi for a conference in May. His hopes were to have them sign a peace treaty. But now it was time for his big party at the Capone estate.

As all four sat and finished their breakfast at the Blue Devil, Capone said, "Be at my place about nine o'clock sharp. Wear your best and look sharp. Most of the people will be big shots. We wanta put on a good show."

"Flo," said Capone, "make sure your girls are ready and in a pleasurable mood."

"I'll tell them, Al," Flo assured him.

Capone looked across the table, finishing his last bite of breakfast, and said to Abe, "You know, Abe, we hardly need these things at all down here in Miami." At that moment Capone pulled out his .38 caliber pistol, pointing at it, and laid it on the table.

"We don't need this kind of hardware down here. It's quiet and calm. Nobody seems to be mad like in Chicago," Capone insisted.

"Yeah, I know what you mean, Al," said Abe as he pulled his automatic out of his holster. "I couldn't live without this thing. No way!" insisted Abe, pointing it towards a customer up at the bar.

"Listen," said Capone, "I've got some shopping to do for my party. I'll see ya later."

After Capone left the Blue Devil, Abe and Ray went out to their car and drove off for downtown Miami. They wanted to check out some big hotels like the Pershing on First Street and maybe the Cortez just across the street. They had heard that Dade County was wide open for illegal underworld activities from a source they got from a blind pig owner who had been hanging around the Blue Devil.

The two Purples checked out a good many hotels and speak-easies that day and were completely satisfied that the county was open for just about anything illegal.

For the next couple days, Abe and Ray stayed close to the Blue Devil. Business was booming and Flo was very willing to please the Bernstein brothers with her sexual ways after closing time.

The weekend had rolled around, and Capone was ready for his big bash. His invitations were out; he had all his guards ready and posted around his grounds; extra butlers and maids had been hired especially for the party, and even Flo was ready with all her prostitutes.

The Purples were ready. All they had to do was change into their new suits that had been bought purposely for Capone's party.

Scarface had invited reporters and press photographers from the Miami Herald. He wanted his party to hit the front page of the newspaper. Capone was like that. He loved publicity even back in Chicago.

On Saturday night, March 5, 1929, Capone was to become the new king-pin of Miami, Florida. After this night was over, he calculated, he would have all the big brass in the police department, all the top city officials, and all the federal agents in Miami eating out of his hands. Pay-off time was coming up. It was now time for Scarface Al Capone to become head man of big-time crime in the playland city of Miami. Lucky Luciano would be number-two man, but that would not bother Luciano. He only wanted a small portion of the take in Miami. His main interest was in the big one, New York City.

On Capone's big day, he awoke in his terrace bedroom overlooking the blue-green waters of the Atlantic to a beautiful sunny day. He could feel a gentle tropical breeze as he walked to the edge of his terrace. Capone strolled back over to his desk, pushed a button, and shortly afterwards a nice, trim-looking maid brought him a warm breakfast on a tray.

As the maid sat the tray on Capone's desktop, she said, "Hope you have a nice party tonight, Mr. Capone."

Capone smiled a little and replied, "Thank you, doll."

He quickly ate and dressed. Scarface had a big day ahead of him. He wanted to make sure everything was set up. He took all day making sure of it. Especially his guards. He double checked to see if all his guards had submachine guns. If there was to be trouble, he wanted the place well protected.

Capone had recently received reports that Cuban gangs had been forming in Miami. From some of his street informants he had information that some deported criminals from Cuba were taking over some of the hot areas that Capone wanted. These criminals were involved mostly in dope smuggling. Scarface wanted no part of dope infesting his new territory. It would interfere too much with his other illegal practices. He informed his guards to keep a sharp lookout for any strange-looking people that might be wandering around close to his estate.

Capone went down to the beach that day to take in the bright sunshine. It was a beautiful day for a swim in the ocean and to get a little tan. He invited a few of his girls who had showed up from another part of town to join him on the beach.

Scarface's estate was only about five hundred feet from a sandy white private beach that had a badminton court and horseshoe pits. Colorful beach tables and chairs were available for relaxation.

Capone lay down on a soft deck chair with one of his young beauties at each side keeping him well supplied with tropical cocktails. The girls were laughing and giggling, jumping in the big waves as they came in on the surf. All in all, they were having a hilarious time.

As Scarface took a glance toward his estate, he could see the Bernstein brothers and Luciano coming toward the beach in swim clothes.

Capone yelled, "Come on, you lugs, join in the fun!"

Three young girls dressed in scanty bathing attire ran up to the three mobsters and pulled them to the surf. When a big wave hit, they pushed all three into the water. Suddenly, three tough guys became little children as they splashed in the warm waters of the Atlantic.

Abe finally said, "Wow! You wouldn't know it, but back in Detroit it's snowing. This is great. The water is so warm and clear."

"Enjoy it while you can," yelled Capone, standing in the surf. "Tomorrow is another day. We don't know what's in store. Live! Enjoy! Be happy!" he insisted, waving his arms about.

After a good afternoon of swimming and relaxing on the beach, all four mobsters went to the nearby bathhouse and showered. Soon they would be enjoying the great celebration Capone had been planning for some time.

As Capone was upstairs getting dressed for the gala event, big limousines were already driving up to the estate. It was only about 8:30 when Capone looked out his bedroom window and noticed Jim McLane step out of one of the big automobiles. He was the newly-elected Chief of Police of the city of Miami.

Next, a big, grey-haired man with a very beautiful wife arrived. He was a big community leader. As Capone kept dressing, he took extra care that he looked good.

Another big-wig drove up. It was Miami's hot shot Safety Director, Bobby Fast Gun Postorri. He was noted to have killed a few well-known criminals at a strip joint in Miami Beach a few years back. The killings received a lot of publicity in the newspapers. Employees in the department started calling him Fast Gun.

Soon, photographers and reporters arrived from papers in and around Miami. The photographers started flashing their cameras as they took pictures of the notables arriving in their big limousines. Reporters started asking questions of the guests.

It was getting close to nine bells, and Scarface Al went downstairs to greet his guests, who he figured in time would be doing him favors in his underworld empire.

As Capone reached the bottom of the stairway, he quickly grabbed a glass of champagne that a butler had offered him off a tray.

Luciano came up to Capone and introduced to him several prominent city and county judges.

Crowds started to form as all the notables gathered in the spacious rooms of Capone's estate. He had music playing from a hired musical trio that he liked from a previous club he had visited earlier in the week. It was indeed a stupendous affair. Even Capone himself was fascinated.

Abe and Ray Bernstein along with Flo and her select prostitutes arrived at about 9:30.

Scarface greeted them at the door and asked, "Where have you been?"

"We had a little trouble on the road," answered Abe.

"There were some Cuban-looking guys that just about ran us off the road," Flo said in an excited tone of voice. Abe pulled out his gun and shot their tires out. They acted like they wanted to kill us," continued Flo.

"Well, you're here now, so everything is okay," said Capone without overlooking the idea it might mean trouble later on.

They quickly joined the crowd inside and forgot their trouble on the road.

All through the night, Scarface kept his party in good spirits with plenty of champagne and the finest in cuisine. In the main dining room a large, long table was filled with the finest and best looking seafood available: big portions of roast beef, whole roasted turkeys and dozens of varieties of desserts. People ate, talked, drank and danced till midnight.

About half past midnight, Capone went outside on a nearby terrace to smoke a cigarette and look at the full moon. Suddenly, a pistol shot rang out. Scarface immediately pulled out his German made Luger and ran to one of his guards. By that time he heard the rat-tat-tat-tat of a submachine gun (better known as the Chicago typewriter).

The Bernstein brothers were standing close by the terrace talking to Jim McLane, the police chief, when they heard the gunfire bursts. Abe and Ray both pulled out their handguns and raced to where the action was taking place.

A Cuban gang from Miami called the La Contra Gang was trying to raid the place and kill anybody in sight. The

La Contra Gang didn't like Capone's men muscling in on their territory in Miami.

Scarface started yelling, "Son of a bitch! Chicago! Just like Chicago, all over again! Damn Cuban slobs! Spicks! Kill 'em all. Kill 'em all till they're dead."

Capone was in a rage as he himself fired at the gang and kept yelling to his guards, "Shoot to kill! Kill the bastards!" That was Scarface's motto: Always shoot to kill.

After the smoke had settled, there were three dead gang members, all Cubans. The rest got away into the dark of the night.

When the mobsters all got back inside, Capone tried to compose and relax his notable visitors. Music started playing again and he ordered more champagne. Corks started popping all over the place. Soon everyone was calm again and the party was in full swing.

It was getting late, into the wee hours of the morning. Some of the party-goers had left, but some of the bigger drinkers were still dancing to the tune of Dixieland jazz.

As Capone's big celebration came to an end, most of his guests had already left the estate. Capone grabbed one of his favorite prostitutes, who was drinking out of a big champagne bottle, by the waist and dragged her upstairs to his bedroom. Scarface finished the evening off with complete satisfaction.

For the next few months, Scarface had his power struggle underway in the Miami area. Abe and Ray Bernstein had their little world going at the Blue Devil with Flo. With Capone's and Luciano's power in Miami coupled with the Bernstein brothers' strong-arm tactics, the mobsters had the underworld under prosperous control in the so-called Gold Coast region of Miami.

Once in a while, the Cuban mobs would cause them

trouble, but most of the time the Capone mob and the Purples could match up to anything the Spicks could dish out.

Six

National Crime Syndicate Conference

Atlantic City, New Jersey

It was time for Scarface Al to plan for the national crime syndicate's conference in Atlantic City. On May 14, 1929, Alphonse Scarface Capone made a big mistake by not taking his plane to Atlantic City. Instead, Scarface along with Luciano and the two Purples, Abe and Ray, took a train.

While the four mobsters were streaking up the East Coast on a northbound train to Atlantic City, New Jersey, Capone's private plane was in Cuba, picking up a load of illegal Jamaican rum.

After arriving in Atlantic City later that day, the four mobsters rented rooms at the President Hotel near the Boardwalk. As their taxi pulled up to the hotel, they could see the big crowds of people walking the Boardwalk and people on the beach. Atlantic City over the years had been called an amusement factory, and in truth the city's major industry was the entertainment of visitors who each year would flock by the millions to its beaches and Boardwalk. The Boardwalk was more than five miles long, lined by extravagant souvenir shops, shooting galleries and side shows.

Finally, the mobsters got settled in their hotel rooms on the first floor. They preferred the lower floors, for they might have to exit rather in a hurry.

After relaxing for a while, they went down to the main lobby and then to the hotel restaurant. As they sat down at a dinner table, they noticed they could see out across the Boardwalk and the Atlantic Ocean. It was warm outside and people seemed to be in a happy mood. Kids were running up and down the Boardwalk. Spring was in the air.

Suddenly, Abe's keen eyes noticed something different moving around out there.

"Look," he said, "down there by that souvenir shop. Those two guys standing there. Feds! I can spot 'em a mile away. We've gotta be careful," Abe said to the other mobsters.

They ordered a good seafood dinner, ate and left the restaurant. They wanted to check out a big house that Capone had rented earlier in the month for the national crime conference.

The house was more like a mansion. It was a huge building with a large convention hall located close to the street. When their taxi turned a corner on Boston Avenue, they could see it wasn't far from the Boardwalk.

Capone stepped out of the taxi and onto the sidewalk and said in a loud voice, "Not bad! Not bad! This spot is fine. Any trouble arises with the cops, we can get out of here in a hurry."

"That's right, Al," Abe agreed. "This place is fine. Our meeting will take place here in good order."

Soon the four men went back to their hotel to sleep and rest for the big conference the next day.

Early in the morning of May 15, 1929, mob leaders by the dozens were coming into Atlantic City by train and automobile. One week prior, each leader had received a letter from Al Capone explaining where to come and what to expect.

Around eight o'clock that morning, Capone, Luciano and the two Purples arrived at the Boston Avenue location. Abe quickly cased the grounds surrounding the house to see if any cops were around. Lots of mob leaders had already arrived. Scarface started placing guards with guns ready at various points. He ordered a couple of mobsters to walk the Boardwalk and signal if there were any cops getting too close to their meeting place.

About nine o'clock, Capone brought the meeting to order. Close to fifty mob leaders were sitting around a long row of conference tables. The meeting appeared to be like a big board meeting of a large corporation.

As Scarface looked at all the members with intensity, he noticed that many of the newer members were from the Cosa Nostra, the big Mafia gangs from Sicily. Capone brought the meeting to order by tapping a water glass with his fork.

"Welcome! Welcome, brothers of the national crime syndicate. As I look around, I see many old faces and I see lots of new ones.

"Gentlemen, this meeting is to bring about peace among us. Let's talk—talk about our problems between us. Let's make peace. That's what this meeting is all about.

"So, gentlemen, I turn this meeting over to you, my fellow brothers."

At that point, some mumbling voices could be heard.

Finally, a member stood up. He was a mob leader from New York City, Joe The Boss Masseria.

At that moment, Lucky Luciano quickly straightened up in his chair, as the Masseria gang was sharing part of a territory with Luciano in New York City. These two mobs were having rival wars over the control of the New York Mafia.

Joe The Boss Masseria spoke: "There's too much killing going on. We're killing each other like mad dogs. We've got to stop the killing among our own kind," he insisted.

Some of the members started grumbling, and another mobster at the far end of the big table said, "We've got to agree on territories."

Capone replied, "That's right, men. That's what this meeting is all about. Peace among us. That's what we must have to survive."

After more discussion among the mobsters and a few flared tempers, all the members agreed to a peace treaty. Somewhere around noon the meeting broke off. Members quickly disappeared from the area.

Capone was happy. On the way back to their hotel, he shed a little tear as he told his mob pals, "Thank God the killing is over. I hope." It seemed to be one of Scarface Al's weaker moments. He certainly never had very many. He might have been remembering his mother when he was a child.

The four mobsters left Boston Avenue and headed for downtown in a borrowed car that would take them to the President Hotel where they were staying. They talked about what they had to do and when they would be heading off.

Capone told Luciano and the Purples that he had to travel back to the Windy City to take care of some unfinished business. The Purples wanted to return to Detroit and to Cleveland to spread the news around concerning the underworld peace treaty. Luciano said he would drive them over to the Penn railroad station on the corner of Arctic and Arkansas.

Luciano had been away from New York City since last November, when he was arrested and dismissed on the suspicion of murdering gambler Arnold Rothstein. Luciano would drive back to Manhattan. Once there, he would become Mafia chief of New York City and still run his operations in Miami during his regular visits with Capone in the winter months. He liked Florida and the subtropical climate with its relaxing beaches and the exciting nightlife.

After the mobsters checked out of the hotel, Luciano drove Capone and the two brothers to the Penn Station. Scarface and the Bernsteins bought their train tickets. All three had seats in a first-class Pullman car to Philly, where Scarface would transfer onto a Baltimore & Ohio train heading for Chicago. Abe and Ray would stay on their Pullman car to Cleveland.

At the Penn Station in Atlantic City, the train was on time, and Al Capone and the Purples said good-bye to their mobster friend, Lucky Luciano.

All three mobsters, Al, Abe and Ray, ate a tasty meal in the dining car as the train raced on its tracks heading west. Next stop would be the B&O railroad station off Chestnut Street in Philadelphia.

After eating, the three mobsters went back to their Pullman car and tried to relax as the train kept chugging away, crossing intersections along the route.

A beautiful sunset could be seen to the west as the mobsters were looking out of their compartment window and enjoying the spectacular view.

Suddenly, a voice said, "Tickets, please! Tickets!" As

the conductor was walking down the aisle punching passengers tickets—click...click...click—it brought Abe out of his train of thought.

In a slight daze, Abe said to the conductor, "When do we get to Philly?"

"Nine p.m.," answered the conductor.

Capone had been sleeping for quite some time when the train's whistle blew and startled him awake, almost as if he had come out of a bad dream. It wasn't long before the train pulled into the B&O terminal at Philadelphia, nine o'clock sharp.

Rain had started falling and it was a damp and dreary night as the three gangsters stepped off the train. They rushed over to the entrance of the terminal to get out of the rain.

"Abe, Ray, you lugs are great," Capone said. "Your time with me has been good. You're tough! I like tough guys!" Capone continued. "See you lugs in December in Miami. Good luck!"

The Bernsteins hugged Scarface Al and kissed him on the cheek, Mafia style. Scarface had to transfer to another train going to Chicago. The Purples got back on their train heading for Cleveland.

Scarface felt a little edgy and nervous as he looked around the terminal. He had to transfer to a Baltimore & Ohio train at ten o'clock. That gave him a good half hour to worry about himself. Capone had always protected himself with other people and their gun power. He realized that he had made a really big mistake by taking a train, alone, instead of having flown to Chicago.

Rain kept pouring down as Capone kept walking around anxiously. He constantly kept his right hand on his pistol inside his suit jacket.

As Scarface stopped at a newsstand to buy a newspaper, he suddenly spotted a policeman coming toward him from inside the B&O terminal. An underworld informant working with the Philadelphia Police Department had tipped off most of the cops that "Scarface Al might be traveling through the City of Philadelphia sometime on Saturday, May 15, 1929."

Capone took his newspaper and quickly unfolded it, trying to cover his face as though he were reading the paper.

The police sergeant came up to Scarface and shouted, "Hey, you! Walk over to that wall and put your hands up."

Scarface had a notion to reach for his gun, but he seemed to know better.

"Spread 'em apart," ordered the policeman.

As the police sergeant searched Capone, he found Capone's gun inside his suit jacket. Capone didn't make any remarks to the sergeant; he thought he would be able to worm out of this with higher-ups.

After the policeman took Capone's concealed gun from him, he said, "We're going downtown."

When Capone got to the police department headquarters, Scarface Al became a subject of sheer political railroading. Within sixteen hours, he was tried, convicted and sentenced to one year's imprisonment, the heaviest penalty under Pennsylvania law for the offense of carrying a concealed weapon. Capone never had a chance. He was unable to contact his attorneys in Chicago and was sent to federal prison at Holmesburg, where most-feared gangsters were sent.

Within ten months, while Capone was incarcerated at Holmesburg Prison, his orders would be carried out by his brother Ralph Capone from Ralph's Montmartre Café, a plush speak-easy near the Western Hotel in Cicero, Illinois.

Seven

Cleveland Mob Scene,

Al "The Owl" Polizzi
West 25th Street

Later that same night, the two Purples, Abe and Ray Bernstein, arrived at Union Depot in Cleveland, Ohio. After getting off the train, the two brothers walked up the long stairway to the Terminal Tower.

Abe walked to a nearby pay phone and called mobster Al The Owl Polizzi. The Owl had just recently taken over racketeering in the Cleveland area from Moe Dalitz. Polizzi was a very influential member of the crime syndicate and a very good friend of Lucky Luciano's.

Luciano had told the Bernstein brothers that if they were going to stop over in Cleveland for a while, be sure to look up his friend Al Polizzi. Luciano had said, "Polizzi will show you some good action in Cleveland. He's head mob chief in Cleveland now."

The Purples had never been in Cleveland before, and their purpose for stopping on the way to Detroit was pure and simple: Just as in Miami and other cities, Abe, the leader of the Purples, wanted to establish more underworld power and strongholds. He liked Cleveland for its geographic attributes—not too far from Detroit, where their main headquarters were, and a wonderful location for bootlegging whiskey across Lake Erie from Canada.

Al The Owl Polizzi had Cleveland well sewed up with his dominance of corrupt cops and sleazy thugs working for him in the newly formed crime syndicate.

It was getting late, around two in the morning, when Al Polizzi and a couple of his thugs pulled up in front of the Terminal Tower on Public Square in downtown Cleveland. The two Purples jumped in Polizzi's automobile, a big, black Buick sedan.

"I recognized you guys," Polizzi said as the Bernsteins climbed in. "Luciano called me at midnight and told me about you two. Luciano said to look for two men wearing purple shirts and white ties," continued Polizzi.

The three men shook hands Mafia style and went on their way to Superior Avenue, then headed for West 25th Street.

As the mobster's car was turning left onto Superior, paper boys were starting to flood the streets, shouting, "Extra! Extra! Read all about it! Scarface Capone arrested in Philadelphia!"

Abe ordered the car to stop and bought a paper from one of the newsboys. With a startled look, Abe Bernstein read the headlines.

"I'll be damned!" he said. "I can't believe it. Capone got nailed at the train station for carrying a concealed weapon," Abe continued. "We gotta watch ourselves. It's getting tough out there. You can't make an honest living anymore."

The other mobsters agreed and went on their way, sitting in the back seat of the Buick and checking over their pistols.

Polizzi spoke up. "I've got a little speak on 25th called The Owl. It's not far from the airport. One of my girls can fix you up with some ham and eggs, and then you can get a little sleep. Tomorrow I wanna take you guys over to a place called Whiskey Island. I've been rum-running off this little island for a couple years now. The Cuyahoga River snakes around up to the island. I own all the motorboats that go out the mouth of the river into Lake Erie and bring back all the liquor I can handle. I supply the whole damn city with illegal booze, and most of the little towns south of here, too." Polizzi was long-winded in giving the Purples a rundown on his underworld activities around Cleveland.

It wasn't long before Polizzi's private chauffeur pulled the black Buick in front of Polizzi's speak, not too far from the northwest corner of West 25th and Brookpark Road. Going down 25th Street, Polizzi's chauffeur was having a hard time passing the city streetcars heading south of town and seemed to be glad when they finally arrived at The Owl.

The two Purples had their ham and eggs, and Polizzi showed them a spare room in The Owl where they could rest for a while. Polizzi told them he would wake them around noon.

As Abe and Ray Bernstein slept, a few hours passed. Suddenly, a little tap was heard on their door.

Still half asleep, Abe answered, "Yeah? Who is it?"

"Consuela. I'm the girl who made you breakfast. Mr. Polizzi wants me to find out if there is anything you would like before the night is over. So, I'm here!" she replied as she stood outside the door.

Abe got out of bed and opened the door. Consuela walked in the mobsters' room. She was wearing an old, dirty tight dress. She had been cleaning up in the kitchen all night and getting things in order for tomorrow's business.

Abe looked into Consuela's eyes and said, "What d'ya want, honey?" in a sort of childish tone, as he could tell she was very young, probably about sixteen. She was Mexican. It was a common sight around West 25th Street to see Mexicans. Many Latin-American immigrants had settled in the area.

Abe finally passed her off to his younger brother Ray, who he figured would be more suitable. Ray invited her over to his bed as he offered her a cigarette.

Consuela sat on the edge of Ray's bed and said, "Mr. Polizzi pays me good money. I'll do anything he wants me to."

Abe dressed and went out to the kitchen and drank some coffee and smoked a cigarette while his younger brother and Consuela got to know each other better as they sat and talked on Ray's bed.

Consuela had a little shortcoming on the intellectual side of life, but when it came to hard work and obeying her boss, the Owl, she knew exactly how to perform her duties around the speak-easy.

Gambling, prostitution and robbery were in their heyday around West 25th Street during Prohibition, and Cleveland became one of the nation's known producers of underworld alumni destined to assume important mob positions in other big cities.

Al Polizzi had a good gambling and prostitution ring in effect around the West Side. He had a gang called the

Mayfield Road Mob that hung out in his speak most of the time. The mob was strong-arming most of the city's West Side neighborhood bars and tobacco stores by putting in slot machines. Polizzi was getting rich with gambling and prostitution. He had a string of prostitutes working for him from Brookpark Road, up West 25th to downtown Cleveland.

The Purples' main goal in Cleveland was to establish terms with other mobsters, because Abe, the leader of the Purples, might want some of his men to locate in Cleveland someday.

Polizzi had a rum-running job coming up near Whiskey Island, close to the mouth of the Cuyahoga River. The next night, Polizzi took Abe and Ray over to his warehouse down by the Flats. Polizzi had a boat dock there and a crew of men who would go out to a contraband ship named *Tranquilo* anchored just outside the three-mile jurisdiction limit. Polizzi's mob would load up their boats with illegal whiskey and beer and head back close to Whiskey Island, evading the Coast Guard patrol boats.

As Polizzi's boats raced off from the pier, he spoke up. "Look at 'em go. My boats are faster than anybody's in the whole damn town," he insisted. "That's why I don't get caught. They outrun the police boats."

Abe and Ray were astonished as they watched Polizzi's boats disappear from the shores of Lake Erie. It was dusk and hard to see too far out on the water.

Polizzi suggested that the three of them go over to a little coffee shop that was nearby in the Flats. As the three of them sat and drank their coffee, Polizzi told the Bernstein brothers how liquor was being smuggled across Lake Erie. He said that sometimes the slower boats would get nabbed by the police boats. The Owl said that Prohibition was making him a rich man, and Cleveland was beginning to realize that a law like that was proving to be a costly failure.

It wasn't too long before Polizzi's speedboat crews were loaded and heading for shore. It was dark out, but Polizzi had the best speedboat operators in the underworld. His boatmen could navigate their way back with their eyes closed.

As the boats pulled up close to the dock, Polizzi shouted out, "Any trouble?"

"Lots of it!" replied one of his boys.

"What happened?" asked Polizzi with an inquisitive voice.

The boat runner replied, "One of those Cleveland Police boats got on our tail. We took care of the bastards, though. Shot a bunch of holes in the bottom of the boat with our machine guns. The last thing I saw, half of their boat was sinking in Lake Erie," laughed the mobster.

"Well done, boys! Hope those coppers have a good swim back to Whiskey Island," said Polizzi, laughing.

Polizzi's men unloaded the contraband whiskey and beer off the speedboats and stored most of it in Polizzi's Flats warehouse. Then the three mobsters headed back to Polizzi's speak-easy, The Owl.

As they entered The Owl, Consuela was cleaning the floors. Ray Bernstein, as he walked by Consuela, patted her on the behind as she was leaning over cleaning.

She looked up at Ray with her big, black Mexican eyes and thought to herself, "I'll get that handsome lug again tonight!"

The three mobsters went to the kitchen and Polizzi ordered his Mexican chef to whip up some tortillas and enchiladas for dinner.

That night the Mayfield Road Mob came storming into

The Owl. They were dancing and drinking with Polizzi's whores, having a good time, when suddenly a fight broke out.

A rival gang from the East Side was out looking for a member of the Mayfield Road Mob, Johnny Bonita. Most people who knew him called him The Knife. Johnny was a young hood, nice looking and wild with the women. He was a Slovenian immigrant. There were a large number of Slovenians in the neighborhood around the West 25th Street area. Johnny had gotten one of the rival gang member's sister pregnant. The East Side gang was after him and wanted him wiped out. Johnny had scarred up a lot of bodies, including East Siders. They wanted The Knife—now!

Polizzi and the Purples were eating their enchiladas back in the kitchen when they heard a scuffle.

"Something's going on out there by the bar," said Polizzi. In a moment, a loud groan was heard by all three mobsters. Polizzi ran out to the bar and the Bernsteins followed. Johnny The Knife had cut the throat of one of the East Side guys. Johnny was standing by the bar with a six-inch switchblade in his right hand with blood dripping from it.

"The bastard was trying to kill me. I slashed his damn throat," Johnny said. As Johnny ran out of The Owl, he shouted, "Nobody messes with The Knife. Nobody!"

Polizzi ordered the East Side gang to hit the bricks—pronto! The rival mob dragged the bloody body outside and took off in a beat-up old automobile.

Polizzi stepped up to the bar and in a loud voice said, "Drinks on the house. Everybody!"

It was the wee hours of the morning when Abe got up from a restless sleep in the back room of The Owl. He lit a cigarette near a stand by his bed. Abe looked over at where his brother was sleeping and discovered there were two bodies lying on the bed. Lo and behold, it was Consuela. Abe left them alone and wasn't too concerned about his brother's sleeping with Consuela. He had other things on his mind, like getting back to Detroit and maybe jumping up to Ellsworth to spend the rest of the summer with the other Purples. Maybe spend a little time with Sheila.

Abe, the leader of the Purples, felt like he needed a long rest. That's what he decided they would do. In a few days, he and his brother Ray would embark for Detroit. But in the meantime, the Bernstein brothers would have much more to see and experience with their mobster friend, Al The Owl Polizzi.

Abe went to the kitchen and sat down with Polizzi, who had already been there and was enjoying a hot cup of coffee that his chef had just poured. As Polizzi sipped on his cup of coffee, he spoke.

"I've got some slot machines and a whorehouse to check out today that are about a half hour drive from here. Why don't you and your brother come along? It'll be fun! It's out in the country where cows live on farms," said Polizzi as he chuckled and smiled. "There's a little village called Chippewa Lake just south of here in Medina County. One of Lucky Luciano's lieutenants from New York City, Tony Rome, owns a little speak down there. Terry Tavern it's called. I go there when the heat's on in Cleveland."

Polizzi explained to the Purples that he loaned out some of his prostitutes from Cleveland to Tony Rome. He also told them he had a lot of one-armed bandits all the way down Route 42 to Chippewa Lake.

"I figure on staying a couple days down there. It's a nice, peaceful neighborhood. We can relax and have some fun," suggested Polizzi, and then started to describe to the Purples what it was like down that way.

"Chippewa Lake is a small community nestled in a valley with a two hundred acre lake surrounded by farmland. At the south end of the lake, there is an amusement park with a very large ballroom.

"The Cleveland and Southwestern Railway stops regularly at the park and brings thousands of people from all over Ohio. Companies and factories from Cleveland and Akron hold their plant picnics at the amusement park. Chippewa Lake has become one of the main resorts in Ohio," said Polizzi.

Eight

Terry Tavern Speak-Easy

Chippewa Lake, Ohio

Later that morning the three mobsters—Polizzi and the Bernstein brothers—got in the Owl's black Buick and rounded the corner to Route 42. They headed south, and in a little while stopped off at a few small blind pigs and speaks where some of Polizzi's men had installed slot machines.

It was a beautiful spring day as the bright sun shone and a warm breeze blew through the open windows of their car. It wasn't long before the mobsters were leaving the suburbs and crossing through little villages like Brunswick and Medina.

Polizzi knew exactly where he was going. Just outside

the village of Medina, he turned right on a little country road. A sign on a post read Chippewa Lake Road. The black Buick turned down the road, and it wasn't long before they arrived at the village of Chippewa Lake.

Polizzi maneuvered his Buick around and through some side streets. Finally, after making a number of turns, Polizzi said, "There it is, men, Terry Tavern."

It was a nice looking three-story building sitting on a steep hillside overlooking beautiful Chippewa Lake. As the three gangsters stepped out of their car and walked over to the steep bank, they could see how beautiful the view was looking out over the lake.

The sun was a huge reddish-orange ball reflecting on the lake with its little ripples shining like diamonds. Large pine trees formed a silhouette through their branches.

After a few moments of capturing the fantastic view, Polizzi and the two Purples went inside to meet Mr. Tony Rome, as they called him.

Tony Rome was waiting at the main door of the tavern when the three approached. He was a handsome man, about twenty-six years old, Italian, with dark black wavy hair and a physique like Charles Atlas, the famous strongman and body builder.

"Got your call," said Tony in a deep voice. "Good to see you, Al. You're looking great," he continued as they walked further inside the tavern.

They stopped in the main hallway, and Polizzi said, "I want you to meet the leaders of the Purple Gang, Abe and Ray Bernstein from Detroit. They were just passing through Cleveland and barely escaped that police nabbing in Philadelphia."

"Yeah," Tony said as he shook hands with the Bernstein brothers. "Luciano called me from New York and told me all about Capone getting nabbed a couple days ago. Terrible thing," Tony continued, "Capone being in jail. He'll be out soon, though."

"I guess we never know when it might be us," remarked Polizzi.

"Make yourselves at home," said Rome, trying to change the subject. "Let's go downstairs and have a drink at the bar," he insisted.

The four gangsters walked down a long stairway that led them to a long bar that was the length of the room. On the opposite side of the room were huge windows facing towards the lake. The sunset was just starting to fade away and the sky was a dark orange towards the horizon as they walked up to a large window and looked out.

Polizzi said, "See what I mean, boys? Beautiful! Spectacular! That view—that's one of the reasons I come down here to the tavern.

At that moment Polizzi looked toward the stairway and his eyes immediately grew larger. Two of his best prostitutes were coming down the stairs.

Polizzi quickly said, "Hello, dolls! How's it going down here?"

The two gals answered him with sultry voices, saying, "Real good, Al! Real good. We make more money down here than in Cleveland," they added.

"Fine, girls. That's fine," answered Polizzi.

All four mobsters and the two prostitutes sat down at a small table overlooking the lake. It was getting dark. While talking, they each had a cocktail, and the two girls finally got up and went to their rooms upstairs to freshen up for the evening.

It was Memorial Day, May 30th, and Tony Rome was expecting a good crowd at the tavern that night. Memorial

Day festivities were being held at the nearby Chippewa Lake Amusement Park. Crowds of World War I veterans would be celebrating tonight. Many would be coming down from the big city to enjoy the quieter atmosphere of Chippewa Lake.

Polizzi wanted to check out some of his slot machines in the vicinity. It would be a big night for people to party and hit the night spots. He invited Abe and Ray to tag along with him.

His first stop was a speak-easy called Lakeview Inn that was located not too far from Terry Tavern. It was a nice little drinking hole near a cross-street in the village. As the three gangsters walked in the main entrance of the inn, they could hardly believe what they saw inside. Nothing like the more laid back and peaceful Terry Tavern. The joint was jumping with excitement. Dancing to jazz music, customers tossed coins into the one-armed bandits like crazy. People drinking, shouting, sitting and standing at a large horse shoe shaped bar.

Polizzi and the two Purples fought and shoved their way inside. Al The Owl shouted to the Purples, "To hell with this! Let's get out of here before we get stampeded. I'll hit this place tomorrow."

Music was blasting from the band as the three mobsters took off in their black Buick. Polizzi informed Abe and Ray that he had another place down the street to check on. "Hopefully," he said, "it won't be like Lakeview."

Polizzi pulled his Buick into a dark parking lot where a few other cars were parked. The speak-easy was a small, concrete, one-story building directly opposite the main entrance to Chippewa Lake Amusement Park. A nearby lamp post afforded enough light for them to read a sign on the front of the building: Spanish Gardens.

Polizzi knocked on the door and a little square in the door popped open. A man's voice said, "Yeah? What d'ya want?"

"It's Polizzi, Al Polizzi!"

The door quickly opened and the three gangsters walked in. It was quiet and only a few customers were sitting at the bar drinking.

Polizzi and the Purples walked up to the nearby bar. Polizzi didn't know the bartender's name, but he ordered a shot and beer chaser for each of them.

As the bartender poured the drinks, Polizzi asked, "Is Steve around?"

"He's over at the amusement park," answered the bartender. "He should be back in about fifteen minutes."

Polizzi walked over to an adjacent room that contained his slot machines. There was a row of six bandits near a wall. Polizzi asked the bartender, "How's these bandits doing anyways?"

"They take in a bundle every day," the bartender responded. "Business doesn't get good until around midnight. Then we pack 'em in here like sardines," he said.

In a few minutes Steve came in the joint with two girls who worked at the amusement park.

"Owl, you old son of a gun, how are ya?" Steve asked.

"Not bad. Not bad," said Polizzi. "Listen, Steve," Polizzi said in a determined voice, "I think you shorted me last month on the slot machines."

At that point, Abe and Ray were both looking right at Steve, thc owner.

"These two guys sitting beside me are the leaders of the Purple Gang from Detroit. They're good friends of mine and Lucky Luciano, too," Polizzi continued in a convincing voice.

The frightened owner of the Spanish Gardens started walking over to his bartender, a real big and tough looking guy.

Abe Bernstein watched as the two men talked, and he didn't like what he was looking at. He quickly nudged his brother with his left elbow, and then with his right hand reached inside his coat and pulled out his automatic pistol. The bartender had the same thought in mind. He reached in an open box behind the bar, and even before he could put his hand on the pistol inside it, Abe had his automatic pointed right at the big bartender's head.

"Don't move an inch, or I'll blow your head off," Abe ordered.

Ray and Polizzi had already pulled their guns from their holsters. Steve ducked down below the bar—he wanted no part of the shooting.

Polizzi motioned to Abe with his hand and said, "It's okay, Abe. Let's get out of here. I'll settle with these lugs later."

As the three gangsters drove off, Abe said, "I hate cheaters, Owl. I'll kill 'em!"

Ray grabbed his brother's hand and said, "Me, too!"

Heading back to Terry Tavern, Polizzi said, "Thanks for giving me a hand back there. I've gotta straighten out Steve, and that bartender's got to go. I make a lot of money in that joint on those one-armed bandits of mine," insisted Polizzi.

Polizzi's black Buick pulled into the dark parking lot by the tavern. The three mobsters agreed that they had had a busy night and decided to retire for the night.

While the three men were walking up to the tavern, Polizzi said, "You know, we came down here to relax and have some fun. Let's enjoy ourselves the next few days."

Abe remarked, "Well, sometimes you just have to mix business with pleasure."

"I guess you're right," replied Polizzi.

The Purples needed some rest, so they went up to the third floor and retired in a large guest room that overlooked the lake. Polizzi joined Tony Rome at the bar downstairs with some war veterans who were celebrating Memorial Day. A few of the ex-soldiers were dancing to slow music, reminiscing the war years with some of Tony's girls.

It was getting late, the moon was shining on the lake, and it became very peaceful at Terry Tavern. Everyone had gone to bed, even the gangsters. A few dim lights were glowing out on the lake from fishermen's lanterns that could be seen from the steep hill. Most of the occupants of the nearby grounds were summer vacationers who lived in small cottages scattered here and there throughout a big circular park. A few of the cottages were still illuminated, but most of them were dark.

Polizzi loved the peace and quiet of this place, even though he was considered a ruthless gangster. He liked the beauty and restfulness of this quiet little neighborhood. Terry Tavern was Polizzi's little hideaway and retreat. He brought the Purples to a place at which he enjoyed being, offering them what they call in the underworld circle Mafia hospitality: deep love and affection until one or the other has to be done away with.

The next day was a day of rest and relaxation for the Owl and the Bernstein brothers. The Purples were getting a little restless. They wanted to head back to Detroit and maybe go up to the Big Fish Inn. Polizzi talked them into staying for another couple of days.

All three mobsters, along with several of the girls from the tavern, took in some sunbathing on a pier down by the beach. Later two of Tony's girls came down with some food and served the gangsters a nice lunch as they relaxed under a beach umbrella.

It was Sunday and there was a large company picnic going on just down the beach at the amusement park. A big passenger yacht was cruising around the lake along with speedboats and brightly colored sailboats. The nearby beaches were loaded with sunbathers, and the lake with people swimming. It was a beautiful day.

Abe and Ray played cards with some of the girls from the tavern out on the pier under a beach umbrella. While the gangsters and the women played a game of gin rummy, an airplane was flying over the lake doing loops. The sound of the plane's engine got their attention, and they took a moment to look up at the blue sky. The plane started climbing until it was just about out of sight.

Suddenly, one of the girls gasped, "Look! Look way up in the sky! A man's jumping out of the airplane!" As the man fell rapidly, a trail of white was visible. It was quite exciting to watch. Just before he got to the water, he opened his parachute and everybody let out a little sigh of relief.

"Boy, there's a lot of crazy people flying airplanes nowadays," Polizzi said, laughing.

Tony Rome had invited two members of an Akron mob over for a poker game that night. About seven o'clock, a dark colored Lincoln convertible drove up to the parking lot in front of the tavern. Two big-time gangsters from Akron got out of the car and walked up to the entrance. Frankie and Eddie Pinelli were their names, and they were not brothers, merely cousins. Tony greeted them at the door. Frankie was really short and stocky, and Eddie was just the opposite: tall and thin.

Abe Bernstein was standing with his brother by the side of the building when they spotted the two Akron mobsters.

"Abe, look at those two guys. One's real tall and the other's real short," Ray said to his brother.

"Yeah," Abe replied, "they sure are funny looking together. Tony told me they're from the West Market Mob over on the west side of Akron. They control all the speak-easies on the west side of Akron and around the Summit Lake area."

Abe and Ray Bernstein were invited by Rome to join the poker game. Ray didn't want to play, so he was going to watch.

There had been reports that the rivalry between Al Polizzi and Frankie Pinelli was flaring. Recently, Frankie and his West Market gang had been muscling in on some of Polizzi's territory near Strongsville on Route 42 just south of Cleveland. Polizzi was not too happy about Pinelli's aggressive moves in that area. The Owl had sewed up all of Route 42 clear down to Medina and Chippewa Lake and wanted no part of another mob's moving in on his territory.

Polizzi had informed Abe and Ray earlier about the Pinellis' trying to move in on him earlier when they drove through the village of Strongsville the previous day. Actually, Polizzi would use any reasonable excuse to wipe out the leaders of the West Market Mob.

Tony Rome had everything set up for the poker game down in his barroom in the tavern prior to the gangsters' arrival. As the mobsters took their seats and all the players displayed their betting money on the big round poker table, tension began to build.

Ray Bernstein, the bartender and some of the girls working were spectators taking in all the excitement of the game. High stakes were established and a one hundred dollar limit was placed on the five players: Tony Rome, Abe Bernstein, Al Polizzi and the two Pinellis.

Drinks were served to the gangsters by one of the working prostitutes. A bright lamp that extended down from the ceiling cast a glow over the room. Smoke began to thicken as the gangsters puffed away on their cigarettes and the game progressed.

One of the West Market leaders, Frankie Pinelli, was seated across from Abe Bernstein. A large pot was building on the table, probably around a couple thousand dollars.

After Frankie Pinelli took a big slug of whiskey and looked at the cards in his hand, he suddenly raised his head and said, "Wait a minute!" He looked over at Abe, who was the one dealing the cards. "Listen, pal, you got marked cards in your hand."

Tempers started to flare between Abe and Frankie Pinelli.

Abe shouted, "You bastard, Pinelli. I'm not cheating. You can't talk to me that way."

"Oh, yeah?" answered Pinelli in a smart tone of voice.

At that moment all the spectators except Ray Bernstein ran quickly back to the bar for more protection if anything were to happen.

"You cheated. You got marked cards," Pinelli kept saying.

"You son of a bitch!" yelled Abe.

At that moment Pinelli reached for his gun. Ray quickly saw what Pinelli was doing and pulled his gun on the gangster. He promptly said, "Don't move an eyelash, Pinelli."

The two Purples had the two West Market mobsters at gunpoint.

Abe said, "We're going for a little ride, boys. Walk up the stairs," Abe ordered. "I'll be right behind you."

Abe and Ray ordered the Pinellis, at gunpoint, to go outside. Tony Rome and Polizzi stood by watching. Ray tied their hands and pushed them in the back seat of the Pinellis' car.

"We'll be gone for a while," Abe told Polizzi. "We're taking the Pinellis for a little ride."

It was quite dark by now and the wind was howling ferociously. Abe drove and Ray held the Pinellis at gunpoint in the back seat. They followed a little street that went along the lake front and eventually took them to a deserted section on the far side of Chippewa Lake.

Abe brought the car to a stop in a remote area close to shore. He turned off the engine, and nothing could be heard except the wind blowing. As Abe and Ray ordered the two gangsters out of the car, they heard an owl hooting in the distance. It was a desolate spot.

The Pinellis pleaded with the Bernsteins, “Don’t shoot! Please don’t shoot!”

Frankie Pinelli said, “I got twenty gees. You can have all of it.”

Ray Bernstein ordered the two gangsters to walk over to a rowboat that had been pulled ashore. Abe lit a cigarette, leaned on the car and decided to let his brother take care of the two mobsters.

Ray reached in his pants pocket and pulled out a silencer that fit on the barrel of his .38 pistol. Two quick muffled bursts were heard from the gun. Two bodies fell to the ground.

Quickly the Purples dragged the two bodies over to the rowboat. There was a chain tied loosely to the bow of the boat.

Abe said to his brother, “Ray, let’s pick up that big, old rusty anvil lying over there. We’ll tie it to their feet with the chain.”

The anvil was lying near a pile of junk that someone had dumped. The brothers picked up the bodies, with the anvil chained to their feet, and placed them in the bottom of the rowboat. Abe grabbed a pair of oars that were lying inside the rowboat.

The wind was blowing fiercely as the two Purples fought the waves on the lake and rowed out to the middle. When they got to where they thought the water was good and deep, splash! A gurgling sound was heard as the two brothers dumped the Pinelli boys over the side of the boat. Quickly the bodies sank to the bottom with the heavy anvil chained to their feet.

Abe remarked with a grin on his face, "Polizzi doesn't have to worry about these bastards anymore. They're history!"

The two Purples seemed content as they rowed back toward shore.

"Listen, Ray. I'm getting tired of this moving around like we've been doing for the past few months. Let's head back to Detroit and maybe up to the Big Fish Inn where our boys are at. I want to see Sheila, too. I kind of miss her," Abe confessed.

"Good idea," answered Ray.

When the Purples got back to the tavern, they informed Polizzi of their intentions to head for Detroit. Abe told Polizzi not to worry about the Pinellis anymore, that they wouldn't be around to bother him.

Polizzi informed the Purples the next morning, while they were dressing in their room at the tavern, that Capone got his jail sentence reduced to ten months. Polizzi was reading an article in the Cleveland Press that had just been delivered to the tavern. The article also stated that two members of the Purple Gang from Detroit may have been traveling with Capone.

"That's great!" said Abe. "We'll be seeing Capone down in Miami probably next February when we go back down to the Blue Devil. We got a nice little speak-easy ourselves down there, Polizzi. Come on down sometime. You're more than welcome."

"Might do that, Purples," Polizzi replied.

In a short time the Purples were ready to head out and escape to Detroit. Abe and Ray Bernstein bid good-bye to everyone, kissed a few of the girls and jumped into the convertible. They had taken immediate possession of the vehicle when they put the Pinellis to rest at the bottom of Chippewa Lake.

The Purples sped up to the little town of Medina on U.S. Route 42. They noticed ahead of them a Medina County Sheriff's patrol car parked sideways on the road. A deputy sheriff was hailing them to pull over.

Alarmed, Abe said to his brother, "What the hell are we gonna do?"

"Crash right through! We'll outrun 'em," shouted Ray.

Abe tightened his grip on the steering wheel and pushed his foot all the way down on the gas pedal. "Hang on, Ray!"

As their car swerved around the sheriff's patrol car, it smashed part of the front end. The Purples went speeding up the highway, looking back at the deputy just standing there beside his smashed patrol car.

Abe knew they had to get on Ohio Route 2 and head for Toledo. They stopped at a little general store in Brunswick and pulled up to the gasoline pumps. An old white-haired man came out to wait on them. He started wiping off the car's windshield, and Abe yelled out the window at him, "Fill it up with ethyl, that good gas in the other pump. The nineteen-cent-a-gallon stuff."

"Yes, sir," the old man replied. "Want me to check your oil, too?" hc inquired.

"Not today," replied Abe, "we gotta be on our way."

The old man emptied the ten-gallon gas pump and started pumping the handle to get it filled again. He put in five more gallons, and Abe handed him a five spot and told him to keep the change.

Soon the Purples were on their way again. The old man had told them to turn left, which would take them through the countryside and over near Norwalk, Ohio. The Bernsteins had lots of daylight ahead of them, so they rolled along the old road leisurely until about noon, when they stopped at a roadside restaurant and ordered some lunch. The two Purples enjoyed roast beef, mashed potatoes and gravy with freshly baked cherry pie and coffee. After all, they were in farm country and that's where home cooking is at its best.

After a short while, Abe and Ray came out of the little country restaurant. Abe, patting his stomach, said in a satisfied voice, "Boy! These farmers sure have good cookin'. That cherry pie—I could've eaten a whole pie!" insisted Abe.

"I don't think I ever ate such good food as that," remarked Ray.

As the two brothers rambled along the highway towards the city of Norwalk, they could see large open fields in the distance with farmers leading teams of horses plowing the ground. Not too often they would spot a farm tractor in the fields.

Depression was weighing heavily on the land. Hard times were setting in on the country and people were feeling the grip. The New York City stock market was falling and a gloomy era was about to appear across the land: the Great Depression. The Roaring '20s, it seemed, were about to come to an end.

As Abe sat driving the car, he seemed to sense this change coming about, even though he was more of a ruthless and corrupt killer than a philosopher of life. Abe took a sharp turn in the road and noticed a road sign ahead that read: Norwalk 10 miles, Toledo 45 miles.

Ray was just waking from a little nap, and Abe said to him, "Only a few more miles and we'll be in downtown Norwalk. We're going to keep movin' until we get to Detroit." Abe seemed determined to get out of Ohio and maybe hightail it up north to the Big Fish Inn.

The late afternoon sun was getting closer to the horizon when Abe stopped at a little store to buy a pack of Camels and a newspaper. As he walked inside the store, a few people, mostly local farmers, were standing around shooting the breeze with the owner, who stood behind the counter.

Abe spoke to the store clerk. "Take a pack of Camels, some matches and one of those newspapers lying over there." The clerk and the others looked at Abe rather strangely. The locals could tell he was different.

Abe threw a dollar bill on the counter, rushed outside to his automobile and sped off.

A little alarmed by Abe's behavior, Ray asked, "What's the rush, Abe?"

"Those people back there. They were looking at me weird," answered Abe in a strange voice. "Ray, open up this paper and check out the front page," Abe demanded.

Ray glanced over the front page and said, "Yeah, Abe, here's an article."

"Read it!" Abe insisted. "Tell me what it says."

Ray started reading:

Two Akron mob leaders missing. Suspected foul play between two rival mobs. Al The Owl Polizzi from Cleveland and two leaders from the West Market mob have disappeared, according to Akron Police Department reports. Possible kidnapping by loaned mob members from the Purple Gang of Detroit. Two leaders from the Purples have been sighted in the Cleveland area for some time.

These ruthless gangsters were spotted by Philadelphia police traveling with Al Scarface Capone when Capone was arrested in that city on a weapons charge.

"That's enough!" said Abe. "How in the hell does the newspaper know so much about us?"

"I don't know," answered Ray, feeling somewhat confused.

The two Purple leaders, alarmed by the news report, decided they should keep moving fast toward Detroit. The Purples were receiving more widespread news coverage now and were more aware of the need to keep themselves under cover.

A summer rainstorm had popped up while they were driving through Toledo, and large raindrops were splashing against the windshield. Abe turned on the wipers, and just as he did so, a huge flash of lightning struck out of the darkened sky as they passed over a long bridge crossing the Maumee River. Just a few miles ahead they would be crossing over the state line into Michigan.

Abe knew that there would be a Michigan State Inspector at the crossing point. He told his brother not to worry, for they usually check just for foodstuffs and plants. Michigan did not want plant diseases carried over into their state.

Ray became a little nervous when they came to the checkpoint. Abe spoke casually, saying, "Ray, take your hand away from your pistol. It'll be all right. Nobody will recognize us."

"Can't be too sure, Abe," Ray nervously said to his brother.

The State Inspector looked at them strangely, but that didn't alarm the leaders of the Purple Gang. People had been looking at them strangely all their lives. They were the Purples, ruthless, tough and considered wise guys.

It was getting close to midnight and Abe was becoming tired of driving. Ray took over the wheel while Abe tried to catch a few winks. They were driving through Wyandot, a southern suburb of Detroit, when Ray noticed a flashing red light in his rear view mirror. Ray nudged his sleeping brother and shouted at him, "Damn it, Abe, looks like a police car behind us with its red light flashing."

The police car got a little closer to the gangsters' car and turned on its siren. "Floor it!" screamed Abe. "We'll outrun 'em. This baby's a Lincoln. It'll even outrun a Caddy."

Ray turned off onto a side road and floored the accelerator. He glanced at the speedometer and it soon registered seventy-five miles an hour. The police and the gangsters were on a chase down an open stretch of highway. It was still raining a little and visibility wasn't the best.

Abe finally said, "Son of a bitch! I'm gonna blow 'em sky high!" The two Pinelli boys had a Thompson machine gun mounted on the back side of the passenger's seat. Most gangsters during the Prohibition Era carried lots of firearms in their automobiles. Abe grabbed the machine gun, leaned out the passenger's side window and started spraying the police car with a barrage of bullets. The police fired a few shots, but Abe had the upper hand with the submachine gun. In moments the machine gun bullets had riddled the front tires of the police car. The police car started to weave from side to side and shortly rolled over. It went crashing and burning down a small ravine.

The two brothers looked behind them and saw a bright glow in the sky and in a short moment heard a tremendous explosion.

"Got the damn fools!" Abe shouted as he kept a tight grip on the machine gun. "Nobody messes with the Purples—nobody!"

It was about 1:30 on Abe's pocket watch when they arrived at the Collingwood Manor Apartments. The return trip to Detroit had been rough, and the Purples were relieved to be back at their headquarters.

It seemed that the two Purples got back at a very bad time. While Abe and Ray were gone from Detroit, some of the gang members were having trouble surviving. Many of the mobs in Detroit, such as the Third Avenue Navy and the Dago Mob, were having double-dealings and bad debt problems with the Purple Gang. Crosstown mob wars were providing the Detroit Police Department's Black Hand Squad opportunities to make hundreds of arrests.

Abe Bernstein had seen enough for at least the present. He ordered all his gang members to go out and collect all the cash they possibly could from all their underworld business cronies. Their leader then informed the members of the Purples to meet with him and his brother Ray at their abandoned warehouse on Saturday night with all the cash they had collected.

Abe and Ray kept low profiles and stayed out of sight until Saturday, because the Detroit papers had been running quite a few articles on the Purple Gang as of late. The Detroit daily newspapers were giving crime stories and their accompanying photos front page billing. The police departments and FBI agents were getting more powerful than in the past. Older methods of law enforcement were improving, such as two-way radios in police cars, better wire tapping of telephones and more underworld informants walking the streets.

Abe was in need of a rest from his vast crime ring. It was getting too hot for the Purples to operate their crime activities in Detroit as they had in the past. The head man of the Purples figured it was time to make a move. That move was going to be up to Ellsworth to his hideout, the Big Fish Inn.

Some of Abe's lower corporals wanted to stay at the Collingwood in Detroit. Abe didn't worry about that because he wanted to keep the apartment anyway. His younger brother, Ray, decided to stay because he liked Shirley and she was still living there. Abe didn't like the thought of being separated from his brother, but they had been away from each other before. He felt good that Ray had a relationship with a woman who liked him and respected him.

A few days passed and the Purples met at their warehouse down by the Detroit River docks. Abe and Ray parked their convertible near an alley close to the warehouse. Many of the other Purples walked and took a streetcar to the meeting place. Most of the members were carrying small briefcases.

Once inside the warehouse, all the members gathered around a big table situated near a large door. Abe, the leader of the gang, called the meeting to order. "Men, it's wonderful to see all of us here at one place," he said. There must have been at least twenty-five members of the gang standing around the table with their briefcases lying in front of them. All the members had hand guns tucked in holsters under their suit jackets. All seemed a little edgy and nervous. Police and FBI agents had been raiding the area lately. Abe had guards posted outside the warehouse just in case any lawmen should appear.

The Purples had a very short and hasty meeting. The guards outside kept a sharp lookout because they didn't want to be surprised by the Black Hand Squad from the police department. Quickly, the members laid on the table the money they had collected earlier from their underworld cronies. Abe and Ray counted the money and returned to each man the percentage owed him. They kept the rest and tucked it into a large suitcase. The contents of the suitcase amounted to $500,000—a total of half a million dollars in cold cash.

The meeting broke up without a hitch, and the two leaders immediately headed back to the apartment at the Collingwood. Ray was going to take his chances staying in Detroit with Shirley. Abe wasted no time getting out of Detroit and headed for Ellsworth in the Lincoln convertible.

Sitting in the driver's seat, cruising up the highway, Abe started thinking about the suitcase in the back seat. All that money and what he might want to do with it. He thought about Sheila and how they had such good times at the Inn. Abe felt like he was returning home again.

Nine

Back To The Big Fish Inn With One-Half Million Dollars Cash

Abe traveled most of the night and finally stopped just south of Houghton Lake at a service station. He had his tank filled with gas and decided to put the top down on the Lincoln convertible. It was a beautiful, clear June day, and the temperature was around eighty degrees.

Abe lit a Camel and took off headed for Ellsworth, about seventy miles up the desolate highway. As Abe took a last draw on his cigarette and inhaled, he started to think. He was alone now and could think clearly about more normal activities such as enjoying himself with Sheila, taking long walks through the trails, fishing and just being alone, the two of them. Abe did not want to worry about his brother, or about making decisions, or about figuring out where to hide all the time. Yes, Abe felt like he wanted to feel more normal, like ordinary human beings.

But Abe forgot one important factor that made him different from other people: lying in the back seat of the Lincoln was half a million bucks in cash. That money was dirty money, not clean. Abe tried hard to forget that part of it and to adjust his thoughts on a better way to live, at least while Sheila and he could be together. He thought he loved her, but he was a tough guy and a wise guy by nature, just plain mean and ruthless—he was a Purple.

Abe tried to clear his mind at that moment, for he had to pass a big semi-truck that was climbing up a small hill in the road. It was hauling big logs, on its way to a sawmill near Ellsworth, he figured. Abe went zooming on around the truck and began thinking again. He knew he wanted to spend a lot of time with Sheila alone at the Inn just relaxing and enjoying most of the summer there. So Abe figured he would send the rest of the Purples—George Lewis, and Harry and Phil Keywell—back to Detroit with his brother Ray at the Collingwood Manor.

It was late afternoon when Abe pulled into the long entrance way to the Inn. The tall pine trees were casting shadows as Abe passed by one of the small log cabins on his way to the hotel. Sheila was standing on the hotel's mammoth front porch. The sun was shining on her long black hair, and she had a big smile on her face. Abe rushed out of the automobile, picked her up by the waist and gave her a big, long kiss on her ruby red lips.

Excitedly, Abe said, "Sheila, baby! You don't know how much I have missed you." Sheila could sense something different about Abe. He was acting a little strange compared to other such times. He seemed to be more passionate.

Sheila finally said, “Abe, darling, I’ve been waiting for you it seems like forever.” They both locked in a big kiss again and remained that way for a couple of minutes.

Abe asked Sheila where the boys were. She told him that they were up at Ellsworth playing cards and drinking beer at the Evergreen, a little restaurant where most of the local gentry hang out. Abe was anxious to see his boys, so Sheila and he decided to walk up the long hill to Ellsworth and scare up the rest of the gang.

As Abe and Sheila strolled along holding on to each other like two young lovers, the sky was getting dark and some of the automobiles were turning on their headlights. The two walked into the Evergreen, and way in the back at a card table were sitting the three Purples, playing poker.

“Abe!” shouted Harry Keywell, one of the Purples’ main trigger men. Harry’s brother Phil and George Lewis followed suit.

“Good to see ya!” shouted Phil.

George said, “How’s Florida, Abe?”

“Good! Good!” replied Abe, obviously happy to see them. “Ray and I just missed getting nabbed by the damn police coming back, though,” he continued.

The three Purples shook hands with Abe, then Harry said, “Sit down, Abe, Sheila. Have a beer. Abe, tell us about Florida and the Blue Devil.”

For most of the evening, the Purples sat around the card table in the Evergreen and drank beer and talked, while Sheila mingled with the locals. Sheila knew most of them, because she spent a lot of time there on the weekends, helping the owner by waiting on tables. Sheila’s father was a good friend of the owner when her father used to live in Ellsworth. Sheila missed her father and they had been a rather close family until he got on the booze bandwagon too much and became an alcoholic. One day he left town and never came back. They say he went to Charlevoix.

Abe instructed the Purples to drive back to Detroit in the Studebaker in a couple of days and take care of business around Clairmont as usual. The leader then told the Keywells and George Lewis to be on guard, for the Third Avenue Navy and the Dago Mob were causing trouble, especially near the east side of town where the Purples' headquarters were at the Collingwood. Abe informed the gang that he would be back down to Detroit in a couple of months. He wanted to stay with Sheila at the Inn and relax and do some fishing on the chain of lakes for a while.

Around midnight, Sheila came over to the Purples' table carrying some mugs of beer on a tray and told Abe and the rest of the Purples that she was going to have a party at the Inn on Saturday night to celebrate Abe's thirtieth birthday. After the party, George, Harry and Phil would leave for Detroit.

Abe had locked his suitcase in the big trunk of the Lincoln earlier in the day. He had all that money on his mind as they drove back to the Inn. Abe didn't mention anything about the money, because he wanted to surprise Sheila and the rest of the Purples on Saturday night. During the party, Abe would have Sheila go outside to the car, unlock the trunk, bring the suitcase inside and have her open it in front of all the Purples. What a surprise would be in store, a suitcase filled with half a million dollars in cold cash.

The Purple Gang retired that night in their restful rooms, sleeping away into the wee hours of the morning. Abe awoke to smell of bacon frying—its aroma had carried from the kitchen clear up to his room on the second floor. The window of his bedroom was open, and birds were chirping in the trees. While he was dressing, Abe stuck his head out the open window and noticed fishing boats out on the lake, as a warm morning breeze blew his shirt to one side. Abe was hungry and feeling good as he walked down the stairs to the kitchen.

As Abe entered the kitchen, Sheila was scrambling eggs and said, "Abe, holler upstairs to the boys to come and get it."

"Breakfast's ready!" shouted Abe.

Harry answered in a loud voice, "Comin' right down!"

Sheila was a good cook, and the Purples ate her food with absolutely no hesitation. Sheila liked to cook, and she had a big kitchen with all kinds of pots and pans hanging everywhere.

While the Purples finished their breakfast, Abe got up from the table, lit a cigarette and walked over to Sheila, who was by the kitchen sink and getting ready to wash dishes. Abe said to her gently, "Sheila, let's go fishing out on the lake. It's a beautiful day."

"I'd love that, Abe," she replied. "Just the two of us. I'll pack a little picnic to take along. Okay, Abe?"

"Fine with me," said Abe. "I'll get the fishing poles and go down to the boathouse and get things ready while you pack the picnic lunch."

"I'll be ready in fifteen minutes," Sheila said excitedly.

The rest of the Purples went up to a lake named Walloon. They had heard from conversation in the Evergreen the previous evening that there would be speedboat racing up there today. Both Harry and Phil Keywell were speedboat fanatics. George Lewis went along for the ride.

It wasn't long before Abe and Sheila were out on the nearby lake with their fishing poles leaning out over the side of the boat. They had long bamboo poles that could reach way out into the lily pads that were growing along the shoreline. The lake was noted for big bluegills and small-mouthed bass.

By noon both Sheila and Abe were hauling in nice sized fish by the bucket. As Sheila was pulling in a particularly nice bluegill, Abe said, "We're gonna have a big fish dinner tonight. I'll clean 'em up and you can cook 'em."

"Okay, honey baby," replied Sheila.

The two young lovers fished all day at various spots in the lake where they thought the fishing would be good. Abe spotted a nice little cove to pull into and try their luck. While Abe was rowing the boat, Sheila cried out in a startled voice, "Look, Abe, over by that old log near the shore. It's a big deer!"

"I see it, I see it," whispered Abe.

The big buck was drinking water near the log. Finally, the big twelve pointer noticed company and dashed off.

"Gosh, Abe," said Sheila, "that deer sure was a beautiful animal."

"Yes, it was," replied Abe with a smile on his face. "Beautiful. Just like you, Sheila."

While anchored in the little cove, Abe and Sheila ate their picnic lunch of cold fried chicken, potato salad, pickles and a bottle of white wine. Abe ate quickly because he was famished. He thought to himself that this outdoor life was not so bad after all. Besides, he had his beautiful lover with him in a little paradise on this beautiful lake. It was almost as though Abe and Sheila were experiencing a rebirth. They were lovers, outdoors in Mother Nature's wilderness, sharing each other's joys and pleasures.

The sun was beginning to get low in the light blue sky, so Abe started to row their boat back to the little sandy beach in front of the Big Fish Inn. Abe moored the boat to the fishing dock, grabbed the two buckets of freshly caught fish and headed up to the big porch at the entrance of the Inn. Abe said, "Get me a boning knife from the kitchen, Sheila, and I'll start cleaning these nice looking fish for dinner."

Sheila returned just as Abe was preparing to clean the fish. "Thanks for the knife, Sheila. They'll be ready for the frying pan in no time."

Sheila started baking some homemade bread in the big oven of the kitchen, and while Abe was cleaning the fish, he could smell the sweet aroma of baking bread.

That evening when the rest of the Purples got back from Walloon Lake, they all sat down to a scrumptious fish dinner with fried potatoes and freshly baked bread prepared by Sheila. Sheila also had a cozy warm fire burning in the big stone fireplace.

One of the Purples, George Lewis, remarked, "Boy! I'm gonna hate leavin' this place, Abe. Sheila's cookin' is sure good."

"Yeah, she's good all right," replied Abe. "Good at a lot of things." Sheila was listening from the kitchen as she was getting ready to bring in another basket of freshly baked bread.

The Purples sat around the fire after they ate and enjoyed coffee and smoked cigarettes while they talked well into the evening.

On June 15, 1929, Sheila got an early start on the day. She looked out her bedroom window and saw the sun coming up over the horizon, shining through the tall pines. She looked out toward the lake and noticed it was rather still outside.

Abe had gotten up early that morning, about five o'clock, and had walked down to the beach to watch the sun come up. Sheila opened her bedroom window and saw Abe standing on the beach. She shouted out to him, "Abe, what are you doing out there?"

Abe turned around to see Sheila leaning out her window. "Watchin' the sun come up," he replied.

It seemed strange to Sheila, because Abe never did things like that before. "When you're finished watching," she said, "come on up and I'll fix you some breakfast."

"I'll be there in a few minutes," answered Abe.

When Abe came back to the Inn and walked into the kitchen, he saw that Sheila had placed on his breakfast plate a big red rose with a card tied to it that said Happy Birthday, Honey! Abe walked over to Sheila by the kitchen stove and kissed her passionately on the lips.

Sheila would be busy in the kitchen all day, because she was baking Abe a big chocolate birthday cake. She also was preparing a big roast beef and boiling onions and carrots on top of the old stove.

After Abe ate breakfast, he went outside to unlock the trunk of the Lincoln convertible.

The rest of the Purples came downstairs and had some breakfast. Abe then called everyone to meet in the main lobby of the old hotel. Sheila came from the kitchen, and the rest of the Purples—Harry, Phil and George—all sat down, not knowing what to expect from Abe.

Just as he had always done in the past after arriving at the Inn, Abe would tell Sheila to go out and open up the trunk of his automobile. This was becoming common practice every time Abe returned to the Inn. After all of them were seated in the lobby, Abe said, "Sheila, go out to the convertible and open the trunk and bring in the big black suitcase."

Sheila knew what Abe meant, because she had gone through this so many times before. She was excited as she ran out to the car and opened the trunk. She picked up the suitcase and struggled to lift it out of the trunk. It was so heavy that she could hardly carry it. Once back inside, Sheila put the suitcase down where all the Purples were gathered in the lobby.

"Open it, Sheila," Abe commanded.

When Sheila opened the suitcase, she immediately saw all the green bills stacked neatly in little bundles. All the gang could tell what was inside, too. Sheila was motionless, not knowing what to say or do. She simply stood there with her mouth wide open.

Abe spoke up. "Harry, Phil, George and, yes, you too, Sheila, I'm going to do a little sharing today of my good fortune. As Abe picked up the suitcase and placed it on a nearby stand by the fireplace, he continued talking. "Harry, you get fifty gees. Phil, you get fifty gees. George, you get fifty gees. And Sheila, you get fifty gees. All of you people deserve this money. We're a family. We're the Purples," said the leader of the Purple Gang.

Abe started pulling out packets of fifty dollar bills and one hundred dollar bills, laid them in four piles of fifty thousand dollars each, and said, "Each of you take one pile."

"Okay, boss!" said Harry Keywell with a big smile on his face. The rest of them took their share of cash, hugged Abe and smiled. They all sighed for a moment, then Sheila spoke up.

"Listen, Purples! Tonight we party. It's Abe's thirtieth birthday. We're having a birthday dinner and champagne for everybody. I invited some of my girlfriends from the Evergreen over tonight. Purples," Sheila shouted, "everyone will have a good time tonight."

All five members of the Purples family seemed to be happy and ready for the gala event.

That afternoon they all went swimming and played on the beach just below the Inn.

Early that night, while all the Purples were taking a shower, Abe instructed his gang to head out for Detroit any time after midnight.

Around nine o'clock that night, three of Sheila's girlfriends showed up at the Inn. They were regulars at the Evergreen on Saturday nights, and Sheila knew them very well. Sheila met them at the door and introduced them to all the Purples. They were all young women around twenty and were very well dressed and good looking. The Purples quickly became interested in them, as Abe turned on a Victrola they had placed in a large screened-in porch facing the lake. The moon was shining on the water and it was a beautiful night for a party. Abe started playing some slow dance music by Guy Lombardo and his swing band.

Sheila began to place the food on the big dining room table. The Purples could smell the roast beef smothered in onion gravy. Sheila had put a lot of work into Abe's birthday dinner.

Abe poured champagne into fancy cocktail glasses, and finally Sheila announced that dinner was ready. The other Purples were drinking and dancing on the porch when Sheila made the announcement.

All eight people, young at heart, sat down to a birthday feast in honor of the leader of the Purple Gang, Abe Bernstein. Everybody wanted Abe to give a toast, and Abe agreed. He picked up his champagne glass and spoke.

"I want to thank Sheila for this party. I'm honored that all of us can be here together to enjoy my thirtieth birthday at the Big Fish Inn." All eight in attendance stood up and clicked each other's champagne glasses.

At that moment, Sheila, who was standing next to Abe, leaned over a little and kissed Abe right on the end of his nose. Abe hesitated a little and said, “Sheila, baby, you’re a doll. I love you.” Abe kept looking into Sheila’s eyes and sensed in her a deep feeling of love and respect. Here was a woman who seemed to have crept into Abe’s mind, body and soul. He never thought this would happen to him, and for some unknown reason, bells were ringing inside his head.

Sheila walked over to a cocktail table as Abe continued to gaze at her with captive eyes. Sheila looked especially lovely to Abe that evening. Earlier that day, she had gone to the beauty parlor to get her hair fixed, and was now wearing a special red dress that Abe liked so much. It was satiny smooth, tight fitting and rather short, considering other dresses of the times. Sheila was a knockout. Abe liked everything about this woman. She was good looking, beautifully built, very compassionate, had a terrific personality and loved to cook. What else could Abe want in a woman?

To top it off, Sheila was a superb lover in bed for Abe. She loved and satisfied him until the end of time, at least that’s what she thought it seemed like.

It was getting late at the Big Fish Inn, and as soft music played on the old Victrola out on the screened-in porch, all the Purples were dancing and having a wonderful time. The moon was still shining on the lake, although it was now lower in the sky and it was getting close to midnight.

Harry Keywell glanced at a clock on the wall in the lobby, lit a cigarette and looked toward the porch where his fellow mobsters were dancing. Harry laid his cigarette down on a tray and called out, “Phil, George, it’s getting close to midnight. We’ve gotta get movin’ if we expect to get to Detroit by tomorrow.”

“You’re right,” remarked Phil, his brother.

The three Purples didn’t take much time gathering up their belongings. Everybody went outside and said good-bye to the three men as they jumped into the Studebaker. As they pulled away, Harry rolled down the window and waved, yelling, "See ya, Abe! See ya in about a month!"

Abe shouted back, "Take care of my little brother!"

The Studebaker sped off down the driveway, finally disappearing down the road that would lead them to the main highway.

Sheila's girlfriends helped her clean up a little and then decided they would head for the Evergreen. It was about one o'clock. The moon was still bright, so the three girls decided to walk back to Ellsworth.

Abe and Sheila took a moonlight stroll down to the beach near the boathouse. The two walked hand in hand and seemed happy under the moonlit sky.

Abe, in a more serious moment, said to Sheila, "Sheila, honey, I've been thinking about you a lot lately. You know, hard times are coming across our country, people losing everything they own, depression everywhere and the stock market falling. I've been thinking," Abe kept on talking as they walked, "I've got three hundred thousand dollars cash in that suitcase yet. I've got a plan for you and me down the road. Something we can fall back on."

"What is it, Abe?" asked Sheila.

Abe explained to Sheila that he didn't trust putting money in the banks or letting it lie around for people to steal, especially during hard times. He told her that tomorrow they would take practically all that money in the suitcase, roll it up in small rolls and hide it behind the walls of the old hotel. Abe told Sheila they would loosen up some of the old plasterboard in certain places where the two of them would remember and place the rolls of cash in between the walls. "Nobody will ever find it, except the two of us, someday later," he assured her.

After an hour of walking, Abe and Sheila went back to the Inn. As they sat on the front porch swing, they could feel a cool breeze coming in off the lake. Sheila gently kissed Abe on the cheek, and while doing so, she suddenly felt a strange surge run through her entire body. Her body became tingly from head to toe. Something was sounding off signals in Sheila's body that she could not completely understand. Sheila wanted Abe to feel the same way.

Sheila spoke to Abe softly and said, "Abe, let's go upstairs and go to bed." By this time Sheila was burning with passion and desire. She grabbed Abe by the hand and started running up the stairway with him. By now Abe was sensing something himself and knew Sheila was ready for an evening of lovemaking.

Once inside the dimly lit bedroom, the two lovers took their clothing completely off. At that moment they immediately kissed each other in a fiery state of emotion, their hands stroking one another's nude bodies. Words were not spoken, just mere movements of pleasurable ecstasy. After Abe and Sheila experienced long periods of satisfied lovemaking, they rested in each other's arms and eventually drifted off into a restful, deep sleep.

It wasn't until late into the morning that they heard a loud noise at the Inn's front door. Sheila picked up her robe from a nearby chair, threw it around herself and started running. Abe grabbed his automatic .45 pistol that had been tucked under his pillow and shouted to Sheila, "Sheila, don't open the door. Let me come down and take care of this."

Halfway down the stairs, she answered him, "Okay, Abe!"

Abe, the leader of the Purples, quickly put on a robe. He could still hear loud knocking on the door. He went downstairs and gently walked up to the door, trying to make as little noise as possible. In a nice tone of voice, Abe asked, "Who is it?"

From the other side of the door, a voice responded, "My name is Tom, Tom Clark! I'm the County Sheriff here in Antrim County. Is Sheila here? She knows me."

"Just…a minute," Abe answered hesitatingly.

Sheila was kind of surprised, but she knew Tom because he would stop off at the Evergreen every now and then. She said to Abe, "Open the door. We'll see what he wants."

Abe immediately hid his pistol under an old coat that was lying on a chair close to the front door. He opened the door, as Sheila quickly walked up to the sheriff and spoke first.

"Tom Clark, how are you? Fine, I hope," she said with a big smile on her face.

"Real good, Sheila." The sheriff hesitated a little and then said, "There's been reports of some mobsters on the loose around the Antrim County area. They're supposed to be on the run from Detroit."

Sheila, feeling a little nervous by now, said to the sheriff, "We'll keep an eye out, Tom." She then quickly introduced Abe, who she pretended was a friend from up near Charlevoix who was staying for the weekend, fishing on the lake.

Sheriff Clark didn't seem to notice anything suspicious, so he took a quick glimpse around the outside corner of the building, thanked Sheila and then took off in his patrol car down the driveway.

As Sheila closed the front door, she told Abe that they had better keep a sharp look out from now on.

The County Sheriff coming around checking the area for mobsters kind of changed the complexion of Abe's plan to relax and enjoy some early summer fun around the Inn.

Thinking everything out as he usually did, Abe figured that hiding the money was still a good idea for both Sheila and him. Someday he wanted to come back to the Big Fish Inn and enjoy living there with Sheila—maybe the rest of his life, he thought.

A big thunderstorm came up with no warning, bringing with it heavy rain and lightning, as Abe started his plan and method of stashing away over a quarter million dollars in cold cash that day. Both Abe and Sheila started loosening plasterboard, just opening it enough to squeeze in a small roll of bills, then taking a hammer and pounding the boards back in place.

Most of the money was hidden upstairs in a bedroom where Abe figured would be a safer place, because not so many people would ever snoop around in a room like that. Finally, Abe and Sheila finished their task of hiding the money in the old Inn, a job that had taken them practically all day. After their work was done, Abe felt a sense of relief, knowing he had all that money in a safe place for the future.

As Abe was tapping the last piece of plasterboard in place, Sheila said, "What do you want for supper, Abe honey?"

"Chicken dumplings and gravy," Abe answered with a big smile on his face. "I saw that nice plump chicken in the Frigidaire yesterday when I reached in for a bottle of beer," he continued.

"I'll go downstairs and get it boiling," said Sheila.

Abe started a little fire in the old stone fireplace in the lobby. He needed some wood, so he went outside by the porch where there was a large pile of neatly stacked hard oak. It had stopped raining, but the wood was a little damp as Abe brought in an armful through a side entrance to the porch.

On Abe's second trip, while loading his arms with nice chunks of cut wood, he paused and looked toward the lake. Abe thought to himself, "Will I ever see this beautiful place again? I must leave the Inn soon. The law is starting to close in around here, and what am I going to do with Sheila? I can't leave her alone here. I love that woman! She's the greatest!"

After he thought for a while, Abe decided he would ask Sheila to go back to Detroit with him to live for a while at the Collingwood. He would tell her that they would go to Miami during the early part of the coming winter. Yes, Abe wanted Sheila with him. He would break the news to her while they ate supper.

Just before supper time, Abe had the fire going really well, for it was chilly outside. Heat was pouring out of the fireplace as Abe rubbed his hands back and forth to get them dry from the wet wood he had been carrying.

Sheila had the chicken dumplings ready to eat. Abe opened a bottle of cold cherry wine for them to sip on to take away the bite of the cool evening. As Abe lifted his glass of wine from the table, he said to Sheila, "Sheila, would you consider going back to Detroit with me? I'm leaving tomorrow. It's getting too hot around here with that sheriff nosing around. I can feel it in my bones," he continued. "There might be coppers coming around here quicker than what I thought."

After a long sigh, Sheila replied, "Abe, honey, with you I'll go any place, any time."

"Great, Sheila! We'll be going to Florida to our club in Miami in January. You'll love Florida, Sheila It's a sunny, tropical paradise," said Abe.

Excitedly, Sheila said, "I've never been to a big city like Detroit either."

“We’ll stay at the Collingwood,” Abe continued. “It’s an apartment. My little brother Ray lives there with a girlfriend of his. You’ll like her.”

Both Sheila and Abe were truly happy at that moment. They finished their supper and decided to leave early in the morning before anybody would be coming around.

The two lovers sat around the fireplace getting warm until late that night. They finished their bottle of wine and soon became relaxed and ready for bed. Abe put out what was left of the fire, and they walked upstairs holding on to each other.

Sheila set the alarm clock on her nightstand for five o’clock in the morning. They both crawled into bed and made passionate love until they drifted off to sleep.

Abe had placed his pistol under his pillow and really didn’t sleep too well for the rest of the night. He kept waking up, thinking somebody was around. Sheila would calm him down so he could go back to sleep again.

Ten

Purples on the Run,

Final Stand

Detroit, Michigan

It was very early morning when Sheila heard birds chirping outside her bedroom window. Abe was still sleeping when the alarm clock on the nightstand went off. Sheila quickly shook Abe, as he was sleeping quite soundly, having been awake most of the night.

"It's five o'clock, Abe," she quietly spoke in his ear.

Abe shook his head around a little and replied, "Pack your suitcase lightly, Sheila, and we'll be out of here in ten minutes. We'll grab some coffee and breakfast later on down the road," Abe insisted.

Within the half hour, Abe and Sheila were in the Lincoln

convertible heading for downstate. As they were speeding down the highway, Abe told Sheila that he hated to leave the Inn so fast, but it was necessary.

Before they had left the hotel, Sheila called one of her girlfriends who lived at the Evergreen and asked her to move into the Inn and take care of it for her. The girlfriend was more than glad to move out of the old beer joint and live at the Inn.

Abe and Sheila left the Inn just in time, because they found out much later that a big man hunt was on in and around the Ellsworth area by the Michigan State Patrol and the Antrim County Sheriff's Department.

When Abe and Sheila got down the highway a few miles, Abe turned left at an intersection that would take them a different route to Detroit. Normally, they would travel down through Bay City and on to Detroit. This back woods route was more secluded with many small waterways, lakes and bigger bays. As their Lincoln went speeding along, Abe noticed a few police cars coming toward them every so often. Abe would head for Traverse City and then shoot across the state diagonally to Detroit. That way he figured he would not ever be spotted.

After passing over a lot of bridges that crossed the waterways, they arrived in Traverse City around noon. Both Abe and Sheila were hungry and thirsty. They stopped at a little general store just outside the city limits. Abe had the car filled up with gasoline, and Sheila went inside the store and bought some groceries. Abe wanted to eat on the run, so Sheila bought a ten-cent loaf of bread, a pound of sliced bologna for twenty cents, and two nickel Coca-Colas. It was going to be an all-day trip and maybe into the night before they would get near Detroit. Sheila made up some sandwiches with the groceries that she bought and opened up the bottles of pop.

They were about twenty-five miles south of Traverse City passing by a small trading post called Summit City when Abe noticed in his rear view mirror a pair of headlights closing in on him from behind. There had been a four-state alert out in Ohio, Michigan, Indiana and Illinois for the Purples. All the state highway patrols and local police departments were notified concerning the Purples being involved in slayings in Ohio.

Abe knew he had to out-run the car behind him because he was aware that the cops were looking for the Purples. He found that out back at the Inn. The Purples leader floored the accelerator and put the supercharged Lincoln into high speed, losing the car behind him. About a mile down the road, and after a sharp curve, Abe spotted a road off to the left. He quickly put his foot on the brake pedal, turned and eased the big Lincoln down the narrow winding road.

Abe pulled over and stopped the car, then glanced at Sheila. In a breath of relief, Sheila said, "Boy, Abe, that was hair-raising!"

Abe looked at Sheila a little alarmed and remarked, "Yeah! We shook 'em off, Sheila."

"Pretty fancy drivin', Abe," replied Sheila.

After a few moments, Abe continued on down the bumpy, winding road. He wanted to get as far away as possible, just in case.

A couple good miles down the road, Abe stopped again and said, "Sheila, we've gotta lay low for a while. Those cops are gonna be out lookin' for us." Abe decided not to go back on the main highway, at least for now. He started moving again and kept driving forward down the old narrow road.

Finally after a while, seeming like they were getting nowhere fast, the road came to a sudden end atop a little knoll. Looking off to the east, in the distance they saw a river flowing rapidly and smoke coming from a little log cabin. The cabin appeared to be situated on the river bank, with tall pine trees growing around it.

Abe took a good look around and decided to hide the Lincoln in some nearby tall bushes. "Sheila, we're gonna go over to that cabin and see who's there. Looks like a good place to hide for at least the rest of the night. Tomorrow morning early, before dawn, we'll high-tail it out of here."

"Anything you say, Abe honey," Sheila replied.

As Abe handed Sheila a small pistol, he spoke in a low tone of voice. "Put this in your purse, Sheila. It might come in handy."

The two of them cautiously walked through some thick underbrush as they got closer to the cabin. It must have been close to supper time because there was a lot of smoke coming out of the chimney. It had been a rather cool day for the middle of June, and Abe and Sheila were cold from being outside for such a long time. As they got closer to the cabin, they could see the river running rapidly as the sky was getting darker.

When they walked up to the door of the cabin, they noticed all kinds of animal skins hanging and drying on lines around the little front entrance to the cabin. Abe finally knocked on the cabin door and, while doing so, noticed a small glow of light through a nearby window. Abe figured the glow was coming from a fireplace inside the cabin.

The door opened and a tall thin man stood inside the opened door holding a double barrel shotgun. The man, with a French accent, said, "Who are you people? What do you want?"

Abe cautiously answered, "Our automobile broke down back on the main highway and we spotted a little road and walked down it, hoping to find some help."

"You and your wife, come in and get out of the chilly night air," the tall man said.

Abe and Sheila stepped into the cabin and noticed a little Indian woman standing by the wood stove, preparing supper.

"Come, get by the fire and get warm," the man said.

As they walked up to the fireplace, Abe said, "Thank you. You're very kind."

Abe and Sheila stood by the fire and talked to the man for some time while getting warm. Abe told him that they were tourists from Chicago sight-seeing in upper Michigan and were on their way to Detroit.

The tall woodsman said that he hadn't lived here too long. He explained to Abe and Sheila that he was trapping up near Sault Ste. Marie when he met the Indian woman. He came down to Traverse City to work in a lumber mill not too far from the cabin on the Manistee River.

As Abe and Sheila became more comfortable with the woodsman, he invited them to sit down at the table. The Indian woman poured them a hot cup of coffee. Abe lit a cigarette and offered one to the woodsman.

The woodsman spoke up. "You good people can stay here overnight if you wish. In the morning, after you get some rest, you'll feel better and maybe we can get your automobile running again."

"Good idea!" replied Abe to the woodsman. "My name is Abe. This is my wife Sheila," he said, pointing his hand towards her.

The woodsman nodded his head and said, "They call me Slim. I guess you can see why. I'm seven feet tall."

Both Abe and Sheila looked at each other and smirked a little as if to say, "You sure are."

Slim stood up from the table and said, "My Indian

squaw is making rabbit stew with potatoes and gravy for supper. You're welcome to eat with us tonight."

Sheila remarked, "Thank you, Slim. That's kind of you to offer."

Slim walked over to the fireplace and tended to the fire, which was getting low. He said, "I'm going outside to the wood pile. Come along, Abe, you can give me a hand with some wood."

Abe was a little cautious at that point and answered, "Okay, Slim. Be right with you."

The two men went outside and Sheila started helping the Indian woman, who was very quiet. She couldn't speak English too well.

While out at the wood pile, Slim said to Abe, "I'll tell you something, Abe. I know who you are. Yesterday when I was up at the trading post in Summit City, I looked at an FBI poster there at the post office. You're one of those Purple guys that they're looking for around here. Everybody was talkin' about it at the trading post."

Abe looked at Slim and then pulled out his .45 automatic from under his jacket. Abe pointed the pistol directly at Slim and said, "We don't mean to cause any trouble for you and your Indian woman. My wife and I have to lay low for a while and we'll be out of here early in the morning."

Slim said, rather nervously, "You can stay all night, Abe. I don't have anything against you and your wife. You seem like nice people."

Abe put his automatic back in his holster and said, "Fine, Slim! Fine! We'll get along just fine."

The two men went back in the cabin, arms full of cut wood, and got ready for supper. Sheila had been helping the Indian woman and the food was ready to eat.

That evening all four sat around the fire and made small

talk. But not the Indian woman; she just sat and worked on a colorful rug that she was weaving.

About midnight, Abe and Sheila curled up together in a small bunk bed near the fireplace and tried to go to sleep. Abe was nervous and had his pistol handy under his pillow. Sheila had her purse with the little pistol that Abe had given her earlier. Abe could not sleep well at all. He got out of bed a good many times. He seemed to sense something. He would get up, smoke a cigarette by the fireplace, grab some wood and throw it on the fire. He did this all night long.

Slim and his Indian woman were also restless. They had bunked down in an adjacent room and Slim got up a couple times to check on the fire. Both men talked a little and smoked cigarettes.

As Slim reached up on the fireplace mantle to grab a brown jug, he spoke in a low tone, "Abe, you look nervous. Here, have a slug of my favorite Schnapps. I make it myself."

Abe took the jug, tipped it up and took a big slug. "Not bad! Not bad at all," Abe said, finally relaxing a little. "You say you make this?"

"Sure do!" answered Slim.

Abe remarked, "I could get a good price for this stuff back in Detroit."

Finally, the two men went back to bed. It was about dawn when Sheila awoke. She looked at Abe sleeping soundly beside her on the bottom berth of the bunk bed. "Wake up! Wake up!" Sheila said to him. "It's getting light out, Abc."

Sheila got up and walked over to the fireplace to get warm. She thought she heard a noise like a boat engine humming. She quickly ran to the door and opened it to hear better.

The Manistee River flowed right next to the cabin, and Slim had a little boat dock at the river's edge. There was a big bend in the river just before it reached the cabin. As Sheila was trying to make out the noise, she could see a speedboat coming towards the cabin around the big bend in the river.

Sheila shouted out to Abe, "Abe, there's a boat coming up the river and two coppers are on the boat!"

Abe was already up and out of bed and had grabbed his automatic from under his pillow. He came to the door where Sheila was standing.

"Get back! Get back!" Abe ordered.

At that moment, two Michigan State Policemen docked their speedboat close to the log cabin, maybe about fifty feet away. Abe didn't give the policemen a chance to get any closer. The Purple mobster started firing at the two policeman. Gunfire was being exchanged by both Abe and the lawmen. One of the state troopers made a run for cover to a big log lying on shore.

Abe took a close aim and fired his automatic with two shots. The bullets pierced through the trooper's chest. He groaned and fell backward into the river. The other trooper took a quick rush for a thicket that was close by. The trooper made it to the thicket and then suddenly tried to be a big hero, but he made a grave mistake. He got up and rushed toward the log cabin. That's when Abe pumped him with eight .45 caliber slugs, emptying his automatic. The trooper's body slumped to the ground.

Sheila came running out of the cabin, while Slim and the Indian woman stayed hidden inside. While Abe was reloading his automatic, Sheila, in an excited voice, said, "Abe, you all right?"

"Yeah, baby," Abe answered. "Go back inside, Sheila."

Abe dragged the state trooper's body over to the shore of the river. He gave a big shove on the body and it went into the rapidly flowing water, quickly disappearing down stream. The Purple leader went back to the cabin as the sun was coming up over the tall pine trees.

When Abe got inside, Slim and his Indian woman were standing by the fireplace looking rather shocked by the recent events. Abe explained to Slim that it was either him or the state troopers. By this time, Abe knew that Sheila and he had to high-tail it out of the area fast.

Abe and Sheila thanked Slim for the food and a place to sleep. "You're good people," Abe said. The sky was getting brighter, so they both started to run toward where their Lincoln was hidden in the tall bushes. Slim and the Indian woman just stood at the doorway of the cabin and watched as Abe and Sheila ran off in the distance.

Abe didn't like how bright it was getting. He told Sheila that more cops would probably be on the look out for them. They raced to get in their automobile and get moving. Abe turned the engine over a couple of times before it started. He put his foot on the clutch pedal and put the Lincoln in low gear. He then slammed his foot down on the accelerator and spun out, dust and dirt flying from his rear tires.

Sheila got a good grip on the inside of the car as Abe took off at high speed. Sheila hung on for dear life, while Abe hit bumps and big ruts in the old path, which was really not much of a roadway.

Finally, Abe got to the main highway. He stopped and looked carefully in both directions before pulling out onto the main road. He told Sheila to hang on, because from then on he would be driving the Lincoln for all it was worth. He wanted to get to Detroit pronto.

It was close to midnight when Abe spotted the bright

lights from some of the skyscrapers in Detroit, about fifteen miles away. Sheila was snuggled up close to Abe when he gently nudged her to wake up. She had been sleeping for about an hour. Abe had gone through a whole pack of Camel cigarettes.

In about a half hour, Abe was driving down Michigan Avenue in downtown Detroit. The city seemed rather quiet to Abe. It was half past midnight and hardly any people were on the streets. Abe stopped at the intersection of Woodward Avenue and turned left on Woodward to get to Gratiot, where the Collingwood Manor was located.

Sheila was overwhelmed by the size of the city. She had never been to any big cities such as Detroit. Abe pulled up close by the Collingwood and parked the Lincoln alongside the curb. He got out of the car and gave his body a big, long stretch. He was stiff as a board from driving all day and part of the night.

"This is it, baby," he told Sheila as he continued to stretch, "our home for a while."

Abe picked up Sheila's suitcase from the back seat and the two of them went inside the apartment building. The Collingwood Manor was a modern looking brick building in a very quiet neighborhood. From the front of the building, with lots of nice looking bushy evergreens growing, one would never suspect that ruthless killer mobsters lived inside.

Abe and Sheila walked up to the second floor apartment and Abe gave two short knocks on the door. Abe's brother Ray was in the apartment with his girlfriend Shirley. Ray Bernstein knew it was a Purple at the door because of the two quick knocks. Ray had some of his boys out checking with some of the speak-easies in town, because there was a national convention being held in Detroit by the American

Legion. Lots of booze sales were being transacted in the area. Ray thought it might be his boys at the door. Ray opened the door rather cautiously while holding his pistol in one hand.

"Little brother," Abe shouted, "how are ya?"

"Fine, real fine," replied the other Purple in a surprised voice. "How was your trip back from the Inn?" asked Ray.

"Risky!" Abe replied. "Cops all over the area up there in Antrim County. I think we got out just in time. Oh, by the way, Ray, you know Sheila. I don't think Shirley does."

The two girls introduced themselves to one another and went off into the kitchen. Shirley grabbed a bottle of whiskey from a kitchen shelf as Sheila went to freshen up in the bathroom. The two Bernsteins sat down at a table and Shirley poured them each a glass of whiskey. Abe threw his cigarette pack on the table near an ashtray and both men lit a cigarette and started talking.

Ray took a long drag on his cigarette and said, "Abe, the wars are getting worse instead of better. We got the police and the FBI bearing down on us all the time. Besides that, the mobs are tearing each other apart all the time."

"Yeah, I know," Abe remarked. "I thought these gang wars would get better after that conference in Atlantic City. No dice! The wars seem to be worse than ever."

In Detroit, the East Side Mafia gangs like the Dago Mob and the Third Avenue Navy were squeezing each other out for citywide dominance. Abe and Ray Bernstein's Purples were feuding murderously with most of these gangs, and the Purples were hardly able to exist on the East Side anymore.

While the two Purples kept talking, drinking and smoking away, Shirley and Sheila were getting well acquainted with each other in the kitchen.

Abe finally had a plan to maybe solve some of the

Purples' existing problems with one of the mobs on the East Side. The Dago Mob was the target of Abe's plan of attack. Abe hated them and called them stinkin' wops. Whenever Abe heard anybody bring up the word Dago, his brother would say to him, "You're turning purple." Maybe that's how the Purple Gang got its name.

As the two leaders of the Purples sat talking, they were setting up a diabolical, ruthless plan of premeditated first degree murder, although they certainly didn't see it that way. Just another routine killing in their day-to-day crime world.

The Bernsteins at a young age were heading for a fall that would end their reign as leaders of the Purple Gang. While drinking their bootlegged whiskey and planning a mob murder, they didn't realize how close they were to the end of the line.

Abe told his brother that he would contact one of his old-time buddies, Solly Levine, who now was a bookie on the East Side. Solly knew the Dago Mob well, and Abe would have Solly tell them that the Purples wanted to have a friendly meeting at the Collingwood. Solly thought it was going to be just that, but instead it was a double-cross. The Dago Mob would believe Levine because they knew he was good friends with Abe, the leader of the Purples.

On the night of Friday, June 20th, Abe sent Sheila and Shirley to a movie downtown. Abe didn't want the women to be witnesses to anything, especially murder.

At about eight o'clock that evening, the Dago Mob arrived at the Collingwood with three top gangsters, and Levine showed up, too. Levine had come to make the summoned meeting look legitimate, not knowing what Abe and Ray Bernstein had in their ruthless minds.

Abe and Ray Bernstein and two other Purples standing

on the front steps of the Collingwood didn't even start talking to the Dago Mob. When the three Dago boys got in range, the Purples unexpectedly sprayed them with submachine gun fire. Levine was just getting out of the victims' automobile, but the Purples spared him.

As Abe was spraying bullets into the Dago Mob, he shouted, "You're dead! You're history! We're the Purples!" and the bloody, bullet-ridden bodies fell to the ground.

Within minutes, the Black Hand Squad of the police department arrived at the scene. Somebody had tipped them off about a meeting on the East Side at the Collingwood. All the Purples and Solly Levine were just leaving the Collingwood when the Black Hand Squad came, but the squad of police had the better hand. Along with the police, a group of FBI agents arrived also. Most of the Purples were caught. Abe and Ray Bernstein as well as Solly Levine were taken downtown and booked for first degree murder. The arrested Purples and Levine were held in jail at the police headquarters without bond until their trial date in Wayne County Municipal Court.

Sheila and Shirley continued to live at the Collingwood Manor and visited Abe and Ray whenever they were allowed. Sheila would take Abe homemade pies and cakes to the jail, and Abe shared the food with his cellmates.

Abe and Ray made lots of friends while in the county jail. Their cellmates respected them because they had read articles about the Purples in the newspapers on how tough and rough they were. The other convicts considered them the greatest.

One day when Sheila and Shirley came to visit the Bernstein brothers, Sheila told Abe that he was going to be the father of her child. As the two sat talking across from each other in a visiting room with a glass partition separating them, Sheila said, "That's right, Abe. I'm pregnant and you're the father."

"Wonderful!" replied Abe happily. "I can't think of anyone else that I'd rather have a baby with."

"Don't worry, Abe, I'll take care of it, boy or girl," said Sheila convincingly.

Abe remarked, "If it's a boy, the Purples go on. Maybe forever."

Both women left after a few moments, and Sheila handed one of the guards a box containing some freshly baked cookies. Sheila informed the guard to pass them on to Abe after the box had been examined.

About two weeks passed while the Bernsteins waited patiently in county jail for their trial. County and city prosecutors were drumming up their case on the two Bernstein brothers. Abe and Ray had some real sharp defense lawyers for the trial, but their case was practically impossible to defend. The evidence against the two Purples was too great. It was simply plain and true that Abe and Ray Bernstein murdered three members of the Dago Mob on the twentieth day of June, 1929.

On a rainy Monday morning, July 5th, the day after the Fourth of July, people filled the Wayne County courtroom as Abe and Ray Bernstein, leaders of the Purple Gang, were brought in to be sentenced by the county's high judge.

All the newspaper reporters and photographers were on hand in the old county courtroom. Even Sheila and Shirley were seated in the front row of the visitors section of the courtroom.

Abe and Ray, with shackles on their wrists, were seated next to their lawyers at the defendants' table facing the county judge's stand. The white haired judge picked up his gavel and struck it hard against the stand as the people in the courtroom stood and came to order.

"This court in Wayne County, the State of Michigan, in the City of Detroit, will now come to order," spoke the judge. As everyone sat down in their seats, the big clock on the wall behind the judge read nine o'clock, with the minute hand standing straight up on twelve.

The Bernsteins were tried earlier in the week, and the jury found them guilty of murder in the first degree. The trial lasted only three days, and the jury was only out for a half hour to decide the outcome of the two ruthless killers. Both Abe and Ray were rigid and tense while they sat in their chairs. Now the judge was about to sentence Abe and Ray for their crimes.

Noises could be heard throughout the courtroom. Finally, the judge smacked his gavel again and said, "This courtroom will come to order." The judge ordered Abe and Ray Bernstein, the leaders of the Purples, to rise and stand while he read the sentence.

Abe turned his head sideways and looked at Sheila for a moment. The judge looked at the two convicts and said, "Abe Bernstein, you will be sentenced to Fort Leavenworth Federal Prison in Kansas for life and no parole." Abe shook his head a little as if to say to himself, "No."

The judge, looking at Ray, continued. "Ray Bernstein, I sentence you to federal prison at Lewisburg, Pennsylvania for the rest of your life with no parole."

As Abe and Ray were marched out of the courtroom, reporters and press photographers flashed cameras at the Bernstein brothers. Sheila worked her way over to the two mobsters. As they passed by her, Sheila was weeping, with tears streaming down her rosy-red cheeks. She took one last look at Abe and whispered to him, "I love you, Abe...forever."

And so ended the realm of the Purples in Detroit. It was

quite ironic that Al Scarface Capone was already in federal prison in Pennsylvania, and now Ray Bernstein would be joining him there. Abe would go to federal prison, and Lucky Luciano had been arrested and sent to jail in New York. Later, Solly Levine was tried and convicted for assisting in the slayings of the Dago Mob and was sentenced to prison for second degree murder.

Sad as it may have seemed that Abe and Ray Bernstein were destined to a life of imprisonment, the Purples name still lived on. In late July, a few younger members of the Purples escaped to Cleveland, Ohio and joined up with the Polizzi Mob.

Abe's girlfriend Sheila eventually returned to live at the Big Fish Inn in Ellsworth. In the spring of 1930, Sheila gave birth to a baby boy whom she named Abbie.